CHERRY BITES

CHERRY BITES

ALISON PRESTON

Alison Preston

Signature
EDITIONS

Cover design by Terry Gallagher/Doowah Design.
Cover photo of Alison Preston by Tracey L. Sneesby.
This book was printed on Ancient Forest Friendly paper.
Printed and bound in Canada by AGMV Marquis Imprimeur.

Thanks to the Canada Council for the Arts and the Manitoba Arts Council for their generous support during the writing of this book.

Acknowledgements
Thanks to Brenda Bourbonnais, Steve Colley, Terri Colley, Gerry Cook, Eric Crone, Jacquie Crone, Karen Dudley, Kate Graham, Marc Horton, Catherine Hunter, Dr. David Lyttle, Lorraine Ogilvie, Mitch Podolak, Reg Quinton, Cathy Small, Chris Thompson, Karen Zoppa, and especially Bruce Gillespie, Karen Haughian and John Preston.

We acknowledge the support of The Canada Council for the Arts and the Manitoba Arts Council for our publishing program.

Library and Archives Canada Cataloguing in Publication

Preston, Alison, 1949-
    Cherry bites / Alison Preston.

ISBN 0-921833-99-7

    I. Title.

PS8581.R44C46 2004   C813'.54   C2004-906003-1

Signature Editions, P.O. Box 206, RPO Corydon
Winnipeg, Manitoba, R3M 3S7

for Arthur Milford Preston
1908 – 1981

PROLOGUE

I bit a dime-sized morsel of flesh from the tender cheek of my brother, Pete, while he napped in his basket on the porch swing. I had been playing Nurse with my stuffed rabbits and he kept interrupting us with his constant whimpers and moans. I lost my temper. Even in sleep he couldn't shut up.

The baby's screams when I bit him sounded different from his usual carrying-on. The cries had an edge to them that cut through to the inside of me. I could tell from the screams that this was the worst thing I had ever done, by a long shot. It didn't feel good.

I don't remember the taste of his skin as much as the feel of it: soft and then slippery. I spit it out in the cotoneaster and ran away.

It was July 11th, 1954. A dusty day. Dry topsoil blew in off the fields, forming a mist of grey cloud over the western edge of the city.

I didn't run far, just two doors down, to the Wideners' caragana hedge. Murray called for me, but he had to take Pete to the hospital. Nora didn't drive. As I recall, it was soon after that day that she asked Murray for lessons and went for her driver's licence. She wanted to go to the hospital with them, but someone had to stay behind to look for me.

"Find Cherry!" Murray shouted out the car window as he drove off, as though she wouldn't have known to do so on her own.

She called my name a couple of times, but she didn't leave the front steps. I waited till she went in the house and then I crept home and hid in the crawl space under the verandah. An hour or so later Murray returned and I slipped out of my hole.

Nora was putting on her gloves. She had called a taxi to take her to the hospital where my little brother stayed on.

"Go to your room," she said, "and stay there."

Nora and Murray are my parents. They didn't know how to punish me for a crime of such proportions. A spanking wasn't even mentioned. I waited for the punishment to come and it never did, unless you count the silence from her and the new way Murray had of looking at me sometimes, as if he didn't know who I was.

Right from the start Pete irked me. I had been so excited when my parents told me I would be getting a baby brother or sister. I remember waiting, a little quivery, for them to come home from the hospital, watching out the window with Elaine, my babysitter, on the crisp December day when my father drove up with Nora and the baby in the front seat of the Studebaker.

"When will I be able to play with him?" I asked. I hadn't given any thought to the types of games I would play with a being so small, but it seemed a valid question.

My mother ignored me, just fussed over her tiny bundle.

"Not for a while yet, Cherry dear." Murray chuckled nervously. "He's just a little bit of a guy."

I think my dad was smart enough to sense right from the start that the new baby was going to be a piece of work. He was tiny, five and a half pounds at birth. I had weighed eight pounds, ten ounces when I was born. It was satisfying to me that I had been a sturdy baby.

When I reached up to move the blanket aside so I could see his face, Nora pulled away. Then she immediately thought better of it and allowed me a peek at the baby boy.

Peter, they named him, after my uncle Pete, my dad's older brother who was killed in the war. I never met him; World War II happened before I was born.

The baby started crying and he never stopped. That's how it seemed to me, anyway. His wails were explained away as colic. He ran Nora and Murray ragged and made me want to scream.

He vomited a lot, more than the average baby, I was sure of it. I was also pretty sure that my brother would never be the playmate I had imagined; he was so frail and disgusting.

My parents held him constantly, cooing and rocking to stop his crying. When I cried to see if they would coo my way, it didn't work. They sent me outside instead. In those days there were kids in practically every house on the street so there was no problem finding someone to play with. There was always something going on: skipping, marbles, British bulldogs, work-your-way-up, hopscotch, or just tormenting the rich guy.

We called him that because he had a fussy yard with flowers all over the place, more than in normal yards. And there were trellises and tall birds and fancy stepping stones, things like that. We figured you'd have to be rich to waste your hard-earned cash on those kinds of frivolities. Nora thought so too. I heard her say it.

So they sent me outside if I was in their way, or got Elaine over to play with me, to keep me out of their hair while they dealt with the newer, more important member of the family.

Elaine was all right. She was a high school girl and I liked her fine. She was good at playing and didn't mind when I coloured outside of the lines. That was something that bothered Nora, unreasonably, I thought. I could have coloured inside the lines; I just didn't want to.

The plastic surgeon grafted flesh from Pete's bum onto the wound I had made on his face. It healed beautifully; there was the tiniest of scars. Outwardly, the damage was nearly invisible.

Because I knew that part of Pete's face was made up of skin from his bum, it was impossible for me not to call him "Assface." It was especially mean, I know, because I was the one who caused the damage in the first place.

The cheek bite was the only major incident between us in those early years. I was just four when it happened. My resentment towards Pete lessened as time passed. Other than my calling him Assface as he turned toddler and then little boy, I treated him all right. He wasn't so bad if you didn't count the way he totally ignored me. I tried to play with him, boss him around a bit, but he had a way of looking through me that kind of scared me, so eventually I left him pretty much alone. It seemed best.

Almost as soon as I had done it I regretted biting my brother. It amazed me that my hate could have been so strong; I truly didn't feel it anymore, after the event. I remembered wanting to hurt Pete and I had known it was wrong even as I did it, but it wasn't until afterwards, in my spot under the verandah, that I began to sense the different levels of wrongness. It wrecked everything, even more than he already had.

I knew Nora wouldn't be able to love me, not after what I had done. I don't know that she ever had. I was sure she had never cuddled with me the way she did with Pete. But I didn't envy him. His cuddling stopped as soon as his crying baby ways did.

My dad loved me; he couldn't help it. But I frightened him now. It was as though I gave him his first taste of truly malicious behaviour. Or maybe he just didn't expect it of someone so close, someone he had helped to create. He was blind when it came to Nora, to anything that hinted of wickedness on her part (like not looking for me the day of the bite). It was because of her beauty, I thought then and still do; she bewitched him.

I believed there was a darkness that lived inside of me, deep and hidden. It came out the day I bit my brother and then went into hiding again, maybe somewhere in my small intestine, I thought—there was lots of room in there for extra stuff—twenty-five feet or so of slimy twisted innards. Or maybe it was in the blood running through my veins and arteries, always there, but inactive for the most part.

One of the main worries of my childhood, besides getting polio, was that the darkness would resurface and that the good part of me wouldn't be big enough to control it, that the good part wasn't very big at all. That worry still surfaces from time to time, but only as a memory or in a dream.

CHAPTER 1

It started with Great-Aunt Luce and Mr. Dickson Trent. I understand that it goes back further than that into the past, beyond the first ape that came to resemble my human ancestors, but for my purpose, for the purpose of this story, that's where it began.

I'm not saying it's Luce and Mr. Trent's fault. Or Nora's, or Pete's, or mine. I don't want this to be a story about blame. I just want to get it out of my system. Things happened. And they happened because of what went before; they just did.

It's odd. History is my thing, my main interest. But my own family's history never struck me as very noteworthy until I was driven by certain events to look at it a little more closely.

There are probably smarter things to do than pore over old photo albums and wonder about the dead people inside of them. But I wasn't looking for a clever way to pass the time.

It was a late January morning in the middle of the 1990's and we were having a bonspiel thaw. That's what they call it in

Winnipeg when the weather warms up in the dead of winter. These thaws happen so often at the same time as the Manitoba Curling Association playoffs that they have become known as bonspiel thaws.

I was sitting up in bed reading a book called *In Search of History* by Theodore H. White when I noticed that the paint in one corner of the room was stained and buckling. I stood up to have a closer look. The room had just been painted the previous summer.

My roof was leaking so I called a roofer. An ice dam had built up over the winter and then, during the thaw, water crept inside the twenty-five-year-old shingles and stained my bedroom wall. The roofer drew me a picture, called the formation the mother of all ice dams. He wanted to have a look at the attic, which is accessible only through a trap door in a closet. He borrowed my stepladder and hoisted himself up. I heard him whistle.

"You oughta have a look at this," he called down to me.

"Do I have to?" I asked.

"No," he said.

I had never been up there; there had been no cause. I remembered watching Nora go up, her bare summer legs reaching up into the darkness. This house where I live is the same house that I grew up in.

The roofer's name was Roy and he was a guy who liked to explain things. I appreciated that but I didn't want to see the attic. My dog, Spike, did and he tried unsuccessfully to climb the ladder. Spike is a wiener dog.

"You can see where the water came in," Roy said.

"Hmm," I said. "Is there anything else up there? Anything I should know about?"

I could see the beam from his flashlight darting about.

"No, not that I can see," he said. "Oh, wait. Here's something."

"Please don't let it be bones," I said quietly.

"It looks like an old photo album. Do you want me to hand it down to you?"

"Yes, please."

The album was covered in sawdust and bits of fibreglass insulation.

"I'll leave you to it," I said. With Spike under one arm and the photo album under the other I made my way downstairs to the main floor.

"I've seen everything I need to see up here," Roy said and followed me down.

We went outside to the yard and stared up at the roof.

"You might wanna get rid of some of that snow," he said.

"How do I do that?"

"You go up and shovel it off." He chuckled. A manly sound.

"Do you do that sort of thing?" I asked.

"No, but I could send one of my boys over to do it."

"Will it cost me an arm and a leg?"

"Tell ya what. If ya get us to do the roof it'll cost ya nothin'."

"That's kind of like bribery, isn't it?"

"Yeah, a little bit." He chuckled again.

I decided to think about it. Maybe I could go up on Murray's old extension ladder and shovel the roof myself.

After Roy left, with a promise of an estimate to be popped in the mail, I leaned out the back door and brushed bits of insulation off the photo album into the melting snow on the stoop. Then I sat down with it and a cup of coffee at the dining room table. Spike lay down with his chin resting on my feet.

The pages were made of black construction paper and the photos were stuck into black triangles glued to the pages. There was white writing beneath some of the pictures.

I drifted through the album, through old-fashioned white dresses and stockings and suspenders and hats. Through picnics and haystacks and barn-raisings and camp. Shots by a lake. People seemed very sociable in those long-ago days, especially the country folks. The city slickers seemed less so: a man and a woman posing by their first automobile, a toddler hanging onto a sapling, her only companion.

In the country shots women smiled and put their arms around each other, kids had tea parties in the shade of old trees. There were ponds and food and sheep and hired hands. Favourite uncles and blacksmiths, recitals and prizes.

I knew my mother's parents were both raised on farms. Maybe some of these people belonged to her in some way. There weren't enough pictures with writing underneath. Whoever put the album together hadn't been thinking about the future.

My grandparents had been killed in a car crash when Nora was very young. They were taking a road trip to Saskatoon when the driver of a car heading east crossed the centre line and smashed into them. Apparently, no one was speeding; both parties were going quite slow, but still, it was a head-on collision on a highway. All three adults were killed outright.

Nora was in the back seat. She was just three years old that day in 1932. She crawled into the front seat and when help finally arrived she was found sucking at the breast of her mother's torn body.

I hated hearing Nora say the word suck; I hated hearing her tell the story at all. It always sounded to me as though she was bragging. She said "teat" once when she was telling it. I was just a kid. My friend, Joanne, was there and I felt like dying.

Nora's father's aunt raised her. That was Great-Aunt Luce. She lived with and kept house for a man named Dickson Trent. I never met them; they died ages ago. And it didn't occur to me till it was too late to ask anyone all the questions that I had: did they live together as man and wife? Why did neither of them marry? Who was this guy, anyway?

I turned a page and saw a picture of myself looking pretty much as I did when I was a kid except that it wasn't me. The girl wore overalls and stood in an open field with the wind ruffling her hair. She smiled full tilt into the sun. Underneath the picture, in the white writing, it said, *Our Luce, 1895, at age nine.*

It was a funny feeling, seeing myself that way. I searched through the album looking for another picture of the girl who wasn't me, to see what she had looked like when she grew older, or wearing a dress, or with other people. I could find only one more and there was nothing left of the happy child. *Lucille Woodman*, the white words said, *1931*. She wore a black dress with a high neck and her hair was pulled tightly back from her square face. Her mouth was set in a grim line and her hands were clenched together on her lap. She had no eyes. Someone had carefully cut them out.

I am about the same age now, forty-five, as the woman in the photograph. I walked over to the front hall mirror and looked at my reflection. There was nothing of Luce Woodman there; I was almost sure of it.

My own effort at a photo album was in a drawer in the dining room buffet. I hauled it out now, to compare an earlier picture of myself to the one of Luce as a kid. There was a snap of Pete and me on his first day of kindergarten. Yes. I could have been her, right down to the last freckle.

I remembered the day that picture was taken. Nora had made me walk with Pete and stay to see him settled. Those were my orders. You'd never have known we were together, with him staying as far away from me as possible on the other side of the lane, poking around in the grassy ditches the way a dog would.

Mrs. Judd, the teacher, ran the kindergarten out of her home, a pale pink bungalow; that's the way it was in the fifties.

"Peter Ring," he said, when she asked him for his name.

"Assface Ring," whispered Bobby Cummings.

The other children giggled.

"Pardon?" said Mrs. Judd. "Who spoke?"

No one said a word.

I slipped out the door at that point; I didn't want to be late for my first day of grade three.

There was no writing under any of the pictures in my album. I decided I should do something about that, so browsers of the future wouldn't get confused about who was who.

On that same page was Murray's class picture from 1958. He had taught science at Hugh John Macdonald, a junior high school in the middle of the city of Winnipeg. When he brought his class picture home each year I would stare at it for long periods. The kids fascinated me, with their old clothes and scruffy haircuts. I recognized some of them even now.

I had asked my dad questions about them as he marked test papers at the dining room table after supper: Is this guy an orphan? What's this girl's name? She'd be pretty if she smiled, I bet. What's this boy's name? What's his dad's job?

As I got older I imagined some of the kids smoking cigarettes out behind the school. The girls would undo their blouses so the boys could see their chests. I wanted to be one of those kids, with their scrubwoman mothers and their wary eyes.

When I called them poor, Nora corrected me by saying that they weren't necessarily poor; they just weren't as fortunate as I was. She didn't like the word poor.

Nora was a stay-at-home mum. Before Pete and I were born, she had been a secretary for a prominent uptown lawyer. That was how she put it. But she quit because we needed looking after. Especially Pete, I always added. I hadn't liked the way she made it sound like our fault that she no longer put on her high heels and fancy suits to work uptown.

My mother looked gorgeous in every single photograph that she was in. It was strange having a beautiful mother. It seemed to me that people liked her because of the way she looked and believed her to be good on account of it. She was always being compared to Lauren Bacall because of her husky voice and the way her hair fell soft and shiny around her face.

I wasn't even pretty, let alone beautiful. After starting out as a fat baby I turned into a skinny kid—wiry. I remember weighing fifty-one pounds in grade two. That was probably around normal for my size but I recall envying the kids that weighed over sixty. I thought sixty was where it was at.

And I was covered with freckles—from the top of my forehead to my feet. My toes were freckled.

My best friend, Joanne Avery, had no freckles and weighed in at sixty pounds in grade two. She was my idea of the prettiest girl in the world.

In the summer sun my skin turned brown and my freckles got lost. That was one of the reasons I loved summer. My hair was a deep red-brown, as were my eyebrows. It could have been worse. I wasn't beautiful like Nora or pretty like Joanne, but I was presentable.

I put the two photo albums into the buffet drawer and there they stayed for several months. Then three events occurred that caused me to do a fair bit of looking back and the albums came out again. At first I thought the three events were separate, just eerily coincidental, but before long I learned that they were three parts of a whole.

CHAPTER 2

By springtime I had a new roof courtesy of Roy and his boys. I chose red shingles to brighten the place up. I wanted something to show for the thousands of dollars I spent.

It was late May and I was sitting on a bench in Lyndale Drive Park thinking about my parents. Spike was on a long leash, sniffing around in the brush. I could smell the river, a wet catfish smell. The reedy scent reminded me of the one time I had caught a fish. It was a jackfish and Murray helped me undo it and set it free.

That simple unhooking of the fish was one of my favourite memories of my dad. He had been so gentle and sweet, talking to the fish the whole time, hoping we hadn't done him any harm. Little fella, he called him. Maybe he knew it was a boy fish, but not likely. Those were just the words that fell out of his mouth. My dad didn't go fishing again after that day and neither did I. I hadn't known till then about hurting the fish. Maybe it hadn't really sunk in with Murray till then either.

I miss my dad.

There's no opportunity for me to miss my mother. Nora is always with me in my shame and my guilt. The oddest things remind me of her, even all these years later, when I am no longer young: red lipstick, the smell of it; crowded buses where people jostle against me with their hot breath; old women who forget to hold their knees together.

The first of the three events I mentioned that caused me to do some serious remembering happened on that May morning. It was the arrival of Nora's journal in the mail.

I thought at first that Dougwell Jones had sent it to me. There was nothing else to think. He was my mother's second husband and the keeper of her worldly goods. I didn't know why he chose the spring of 1995 to send it. My life was going okay, with my work and my small circle of friends. I'd even been taking a night course in Italian cooking. I went with Hermione, my friend and haircutter, who has developed an interest in food preparation.

Maybe Dougwell had been going through the last of Nora's things, clearing them out, and hadn't been able to bring himself to either keep the journal or throw it away.

My mother died of bone cancer nine years ago in 1986. At the time of her death Dougwell sent me other stuff, like the deed for our house on Monck Avenue where I still live, like Murray's all-important life insurance policy, things like that. He asked me if I wanted to come out west and go through Nora's belongings. There might be a piece or two I would like to have. He wasn't wrong in thinking I might still be needing something from my mother; he was trying to do the right thing. But I declined his invitation, told him I didn't want anything else, no jewelry or personal items of any kind. I think he understood how I felt; he just didn't know what to do with all her stuff.

Now the little green book sat closed on my dining room table. When Stan, my letter carrier, had handed me the parcel that morning I thought very little of it at first. It could have been anything: a coffee sample, perhaps, or a new detergent. But then I saw my name in big block letters.

There was no return address. The small parcel weighed heavily in my hands.

"Are you all right?" Stan asked. My apple tree reached out over the sidewalk and he stood inside the lower branches, camouflaged by blossoms.

Spike strained at his leash, which I had tied to the iron railing. He wanted to be nearer to Stan.

"What?" I said. "Oh, yes. Sorry. I just wasn't expecting anything package-wise."

Stan stepped out from under the tree. He had a cigarette in his mouth and the ash portion was longer than the rest of it. He approached my dog and stroked his silky brown ears.

"Hey, Spike," he said.

"I'm sorry about the tree," I said. "I'll trim the branches back after the flowers are finished."

"Don't worry," Stan said. "It's a beautiful tree. Your birch is beautiful too." He pointed to the weeping birch with his cigarette and the ash tipped off onto his shirt. He didn't do anything about it. His hands were full of mail and Spike's ears. He was juggling a few sets of flyers along with the real mail; they were sticking out of his bag here and there and he even had one set in the pocket of his unzipped spring jacket. They looked kind of precarious and I worried that they would spill out onto the ground. "You don't see a lot of birches anymore," he added.

"No?" I hadn't noticed or thought about that.

"You look a little…stunned," Stan said. "Maybe you should sit down."

I sat on the front steps and stared at the small neat package. A brown paper bag had been sliced open and used as wrapping paper. It was fastened with masking tape.

Stan moved slowly away down the sidewalk. He looked back and smiled, squinting through the smoke.

I undid the brown paper. It was the first time I had ever seen Nora's journal. I hadn't known she'd kept such a thing. A familiar sick feeling swooped up into my throat. A family feeling. When I opened it to the first page I saw the word, *Thoughts,* written in her hand. Her penmanship was dramatic, with swirls and tails and curly bits. Where had she learned to write that way? They didn't teach it at any school I ever attended. I was afraid to turn the page.

"Stan?" I called. He was leaving my neighbours' yard now, sticking to the sidewalk between their neatly trimmed plum trees.

"Yes?" He turned and began walking back towards me. Pink petals covered his shoulders. Spike squealed with excitement.

"No! Stop!" I shouted. "Don't waste your steps!"

Stan clutched the front of his shirt then and I thought I'd given him a heart attack.

"I just wanted to say to be sure to cut across the grass if you want to. You don't have to stick to the sidewalk."

"Oh." He smiled. "Thanks. I just may take you up on that." He shifted his bag on his shoulders. "I thought I must have given you the wrong mail or something. That's usually why people call me back."

"And if you ever need to get warm," I went on, "or cool off, or if you need a drink of water or anything, please knock on my door."

I wanted to say, if you have to go to the bathroom, but I thought that might sound as though I had been thinking about his penis.

"Thanks, Cherry. Thanks kindly. Actually, I'm going to be moving to a downtown route in a month or two, so I won't have to worry about grass or those kinds of things."

"Oh." I felt unreasonably bereft. I had taken Stan for granted. "I'll miss you," I said. "We all will." I gestured to include the neighbourhood.

"Thanks," he said. "The mail's heavier downtown but you don't have to carry it as far or do so much walking."

I didn't want Stan to go. He had been my mailman for several years. It had taken me till I was never going to see him again to offer him anything.

"And there's more shelter from the weather," he said.

"It makes sense, then," I said. "Well, good for you."

He gave a little salute and trudged away.

I watched till he had dropped the mail in Darius Widener's box, two doors down. The sadness I felt in my chest was alarming. Maybe it was the timing of Stan's announcement, when all those family feelings were creeping in.

Turning back to Nora's journal, I flipped through it quickly so that I couldn't focus on the words. There were dates on the right-hand corners of certain pages and I let myself zero in on those. They went all the way back to the late thirties when Nora was a young girl. And I saw that many of the pages contained few words, incomplete sentences, just, as the front page indicated, thoughts. There were some drawings, too, scattered throughout.

One line on its own page fastened itself in my view:

He seems so feeble.

The date was 1960. She was talking about Pete.

I should never have started with the nickname; it made him seem less than he was. I remember our babysitter, Elaine, accidentally calling Pete Assface once, even though she was always yelling at me for saying it. We were playing in the living room and Pete was showing her a magic trick that involved a never-ending series of scarves.

"*Assface the Magnificent,*" Elaine announced in a loud voice and immediately covered her mouth with her hand. It had just slipped out. She didn't mean anything by it. She liked Pete, thought he was inventive. I laughed and she felt terrible.

Murray was shocked when he heard Elaine say it. He scolded us both, worried that the name would stick. I never heard her call him that again.

I called Pete Assface all the time.

That's how the kids in the neighbourhood knew him for several years. The name spread quickly once it escaped our house and by the time he was in school, that was pretty much who he was.

I said I didn't want this to be a story about blame, but I can't help it. I blame myself for that.

He seems so feeble.

That was all I had managed of the journal so far. Even those few words seemed too much: Nora's thoughts on Pete's feebleness. I couldn't look further. Not yet, anyway. I closed the book and took it into the house.

I didn't know when I'd get to it again. The river seemed a better idea, with its muddy banks and water sounds.

My house is just a block and a half from the Red River. Filthy as it is, the river has always been a comfort to me. I walk beside it, along the path in Lyndale Drive Park.

The park didn't used to have a name. It was just called "down by the river." I remembered laughing with Joanne, when we were kids, because the city had decided to declare it a park. It made it too official, too public, for something that we owned.

We had shouted to kids on the other side of the river—boys too tiny to make out. We chose to make them handsome and worldly, superior to our own boys. And I guess they did the same with us. We would make dates with them and spend hours getting ready, washing our hair and choosing what to wear, only to shout at them for an hour or so, back and forth across the sluggish brown water of the Red. It didn't take long to lose interest. There wasn't much satisfaction in it and we knew better than to meet them up close. I guess we understood, deep down, how great the disappointment would be.

On windy days the water gets riled up and it's easy to see how the force of the current could pull someone under. It happens every year. The Red River claims at least one life.

There is a marina across the way. Sometimes in the summer there are parties on the boats and again, in the old days, my friends and I would shout across, never with much success. These were older kids, or even adults, and we weren't of much interest to them with our questions and comments: "So, are you guys drinking beer? We have cigarettes but no beer." Those were the types of things we said. Very sophisticated.

The river freezes solid in winter, of course, which makes getting to the other side untroublesome, once the paths have been trampled down. It would have been simple to visit the tiny boys then, but in the winter they were never there. We tobogganed, a sport that scared me. For a while I assumed that that was how I was going to die, especially if Pete was with us, because he couldn't see me. It would have been so easy for him to glide over me and drive a jagged piece of wood from a broken toboggan through my eye and into my brain.

I walked back home now, breathing in the scent of the plum and the cherry and the apple blossoms. Whatever Nora's journal had to tell me, I wanted to believe I could take it.

CHAPTER 3

Reading Nora's journal was hard work. I took it in small portions, usually reserving a chunk of time for it in the late afternoon. I figured that way it would be too late for Nora's words to colour my whole day but early enough that they wouldn't keep me from sleep. It didn't always work.

Thoughts was a misleading title. There were facts and events and dates and times, descriptions of the weather. Codes and secret words for Nora's eyes alone. And thoughts, too.

Another reason for reading it in the late afternoon was that I could accompany it with a drink: gin and tonic with a squeeze of lime.

I didn't always follow along chronologically. Something, maybe impatience or fear, maybe both, caused me to leap ahead, then back again, starving for pieces of my mother and then wishing I had never seen her face.

The day after Stan dropped it off, I read this:

July, 1937.
Mr. Trent had his men friends over for cards tonight.
Jack Logan, Herb Howland, and Darcy Root. I don't think

Darcy is a man at all, but she's the biggest and scares me the most. They played on the vranda because it was so hot. Luce served them whiskey and pikkled eggs. Darcy touched Luce on the behind. Who do you like the best? she said and all the men laughed. Luce turned red as blood.

Nora would have been nine.

My thoughts wandered to a morning long ago when I was alone in the kitchen with my parents. I was eating white toast with grape jelly and peanut butter; my dad was eating a soft-boiled egg from an eggcup; Nora was drinking instant coffee. Pete must have been getting washed or dressed, or maybe he was practising card tricks in his room.

"Who do you like best, Pete or me?" I asked.

The radio was tuned to CKRC and Ricky Nelson was singing "Poor Little Fool."

Murray got up from his chair and put his arms around me. "We more than like you, Cherry. We love you to pieces and we love you both exactly the same amount."

Nora got up and threw the dregs of her coffee down the sink. "Of course we do," she said, as if it went without saying. She didn't even look at me.

I've come to know that parents are usually lying when they say that they love their kids equally. They have favourites and it's a lie you can't blame them for. Anyway, I knew Murray loved me best, though he loved Pete too. I suspected that Nora loved no one. For as long as my dad lasted, I did okay. He took care of all of us.

Sometimes I think everything would have been different if Murray hadn't died when he did, if he had lived on.

And the way it happened was hard on us, Pete and me. We were too young for that kind of shock. I was nine and Pete was six.

Murray had been looking tired, his features blurry, lost in the greyness of his face. When he came home from school at around 4:30 he would usually lie down on the Toronto couch for a short nap before supper. He always placed a little cushion on his chest. I guess it was his version of a teddy bear.

One Friday after school I went into the living room to watch my dad sleep. I know it was a Friday because I had Explorers after supper and we were eating early because of me. Explorers was a group at the United Church for girls who weren't old enough for CGIT—Canadian Girls in Training.

"In training for what?" our boys asked us, later, when we were in CGIT. We always called the boys from school *our boys* as though they belonged to us. They did in a way; we were all they had for girls at that young stage of our lives.

"To be spies," we said, "in training to be spies, like Mata Hari, only a million times more beautiful."

"Hardy har har har," they shouted and pelted us with snowballs as we ran shrieking down the lane.

Anyway, that Friday before supper I watched my dad sleep. I admired his snores and the way he could drop off in a matter of seconds. He was an expert napper.

He didn't have the cushion on his chest that Friday, so I placed it there for him, as gently as I could. His eyes opened when I did this and he smiled and removed it.

"Thanks, Cherry, honey, but the cushion feels kind of heavy on my chest these days."

That scared me a little, but not too much. I was in grade four by then; Pete was in grade one. Dads of kids that age didn't die. Sometimes they disappeared. There were two kids at school that I knew of whose dads weren't around. Joanne and I suspected something sinister, like divorce or desertion.

But no one I knew then had a dad who died.

Except us.

It was one week later exactly, a Friday in early May. The crocuses were up in the yard, but not yet blooming. Spring seemed late in coming that year or maybe I was more impatient than usual.

I was wearing my Explorer uniform, which I put on before supper so I would be ready to head out as soon as I finished dessert and brushed my teeth.

Apple crisp was on the menu that night. It was Murray's favourite, not mine. I preferred blueberry or rhubarb crisp but it was too early in the season for either of those. Nora never put enough topping on the dessert, enough brown sugar and butter. That was the best part. I told her a thousand times. It seemed to me her heart was never in her cooking.

She was in the kitchen, pulling a salmon loaf out of the oven when she told me to wake up my dad and tell Pete to wash his hands. I was tempted just to yell out their names from where I stood next to her, there by the stove, but I knew that would infuriate her. Sometimes that was what I wanted more than anything, but not on that particular day. I didn't always feel strong enough for Nora's furies.

When I entered the living room Pete was on the rug in the middle of the floor playing with his Tinkertoys. He was building a space ship. He should have been on bare floor. The brown rug with its soft worms interfered with his progress.

This was before shag carpets. We had what must have been the precursor: a thin rug with inch long protuberances throughout. There was space between them and they were limp, like night crawlers. Nothing held the rug in place; there was no underlay like at Joanne's house where everything seemed more civilized, more modern. I would take runs at the rug early on Saturday mornings and slide from one end of the living room to the other. I had to move a coffee table and a stool to do this and it drove Nora to distraction but it was one of my favourite games. It would have been more fun if my brother had joined in, but that was next to impossible considering the state of our relationship.

"Wash your hands, Pete," I said.

He could hear me; he just appeared not to see me and seldom spoke in my presence. So far he had never spoken directly to me.

Carefully, he fastened one more piece to the space ship and then he stood up and left the room.

I moved to touch my dad's arm. The first thing I noticed was that once again, he napped without his cushion. It lay propped up between him and the wall. His right arm reached across his chest touching his left one.

Then I noticed the smell of pee. I wondered if Pete had taken a leak in amongst the worms of the rug or even if I had wet my pants inside my crisp Explorer uniform. Wild thoughts: we were both long past that. And then I saw that my dad's eyelids were part way open, but that he wasn't awake.

When I touched his skin it was warm. I knelt beside him, but I couldn't, no matter how hard I looked, see the rise and fall of his chest.

"Dad?" I whispered.

I didn't tell him that supper was ready.

"Mum!" I screamed and a terrible clatter exploded from the kitchen.

He wasn't dead when I first walked in the room. The life left him in the few seconds that I stood there looking at my brother. I know that. For a long time I tortured myself with the thought that if I'd come sooner, I could have saved him somehow.

Pete didn't seem to have noticed anything. He was focussed on his Tinkertoys. It was hard for me, to think that my dad couldn't warn me with something, a soft cry or a moan before those last quiet moments. He would have, if he could have.

There was no funeral. Nora said she didn't feel up to it. Maybe later, she said.

A man with very red lips delivered Murray's ashes to us in a golden urn. Nora placed them on the mantel above the fireplace.

I wasn't sure how to feel about this. It scared me at first, the idea of my dad in an urn in the living room. I wouldn't look inside it, in case there was something there that I couldn't bear to see, a recognizable fingernail or a part of his baby toe.

No one else had a dad in a jar; how would I explain it to my friends? I was also terrified that the urn would get knocked over and Murray would scatter. Parts of him would disappear. So I found myself guarding the ashes, sitting in front of the mantel in a chair

I carried in from the dining room. No living room chair was close enough. I pretended to read while on guard, but I couldn't concentrate on anything but the urn.

When I came home on the last day of school before summer holidays the ashes were gone. There was a framed picture of Murray in their place, one of his school pictures. It had been enlarged.

"The urn is in my closet in the bedroom," Nora said. "I think it's better to put it away. We wouldn't want the ashes to spill."

I think my guard duty had made Nora uncomfortable. I went to look in her closet. Murray seemed safe enough in his new spot. I didn't disagree with this move on Nora's part, but I still didn't get it.

"Why don't we bury him?" I asked. "In a cemetery like other people do?"

"We will," Nora said. "We will, but not yet. One beautiful summer day you and I and Pete will take him out to St. Vital Cemetery and dig a hole and bury him next to…"

"Next to who?" I asked.

"Nobody," she said. "Next to a big tree."

This was no good. There were supposed to be other people involved: Murray's friends, his fellow teachers, our neighbours—people who would say what a fine man he was. And we weren't supposed to dig the hole ourselves! That was the gravedigger's job. I was convinced that Nora was missing vast areas of knowledge.

So I visited Murray in my mum's closet, every day for a while, then every second day. Before long it was just now and then. I knew he was there, in an urn in a box and as safe as could be expected under the circumstances.

CHAPTER 4

A huge sadness washes over me now when I think of what Pete and I missed out on by not having each other to lean on. After that one time when I took things way too far and bit him on the cheek, what I felt for my brother was mostly a contained kind of love and, I guess, frustration at his avoidance of me. I wanted to be friends with him, although I didn't try very hard. His complete rejection of me did its job.

When Pete was in grade two, in the fall of the year that Murray died, Nordale School had an air raid drill. This happened from time to time because of the threat of nuclear war. Even I, in grade five by then, knew it was a useless exercise. I'd seen the pictures of Hiroshima; we all had.

My classroom was across the hall from Pete's. I could see his small form sitting on the floor against the wall, arms around his knees, head down. He was shaking, sobbing. I went to him against the shouts of the grade four teacher, Miss Pratt, who was in charge of the drill. It was an automatic gesture on my part; I didn't think.

"Pete," I whispered and touched his back through his little plaid shirt.

He stiffened at the sound of my voice. His body became a plank beneath my hand.

After a few moments I stood up and walked back to my spot on the floor. It wasn't easy for me to let him go, but he embarrassed me as well as hurt me. What must people think of a gangly girl who a sweet little boy hates so much?

Later that afternoon I was called down to the principal's office over the public address system. Miss Pratt was there and she watched with a smirk on her face as Mr. Austin, the principal, strapped me three times on each hand for disobedience. I had liked Mr. Austin up till that day. All he had was Miss Pratt's word that I had ignored her. I remember thinking that he was probably just punishing me because she had great big pointed tits and he wanted to squeeze them.

I saw that trying with Pete would open me up to bigger hurts than the ones he sent my way by ignoring me. But we needed each other, especially after Murray died. Nora wasn't enough family for anyone.

She went through the motions: planted flowers in the flowerbeds; joined the women's church circle; she even became a CGIT leader for part of a year, but she couldn't pull that one off. She had to quit—made up a health problem and weaseled out of it. All her motherly activities were acts, and not for Pete and me, but for the other women in the neighbourhood. She fed us and she clothed us, but I couldn't help feeling it was just for show.

CHAPTER 5

I have never been an ambitious person. I just liked going to school. History was what interested me in high school, recent history, so that's what I ended up studying. After I'd gotten my bachelor's degree I just kept on going till I had a master's and then my Ph.D. It could have been Henry's influence. He was my first real boyfriend and a history nut. We talked a lot about wanting to understand what went before, getting down to the actual reasons that led men and women to do the things that they did.

As a fifth-generation Canadian on Murray's side I wanted to know why men like my great-great-grandfather left Armagh to come to such a strange and stormy land. Was his Irish life so terrible? Or was it restlessness? And what about my great-great-grandmother? Was it love that made her follow? Duty? How hard did she fight against the plan? Or was it she who grew restive? How could anyone be so brave and strong and naive? Yeah, I know: famine in the old country, promise of land in the new. But still. I feel so far removed from anyone who could have set out on such an adventure.

That I come from such stock is a source of pride for me. I wonder what they pictured as they clung to the ship's rail and peered out over the dark waves. How different were their dreams from what awaited them on the distant shore? Quite different, I'll bet.

It wasn't hard for me to imagine Pete on one of those ships. I was physically stronger than my brother, but he was a tough little guy in his way.

He was slight and very pale. It didn't take much to flatten him. He was one of those kids who went to the doctor once a week to get needles because he was allergic to so many things: dust, cats, tomatoes, strawberries, nuts, pollen. It seemed to go on for years, that desensitization process. Maybe that's why needles were so easy for him to take in later years.

During grades one to six he missed many weeks of school with one childhood disease after another. He got chicken pox, measles, mumps, scarlet fever, all the things that young kids got. Nora fussed, of course, but supposed it was just as well he contracted them early on. She wished I had come down with them at the same time, to get it all over with at once, but apparently I had an immune system like Mighty Mouse.

Pete's strength came out in other ways. For instance, he wasn't afraid to take a dare. I thought of it as toughness at the time, but as I look back now, I see it could have been foolhardiness, not giving a hoot.

He stole from Norbridge Pharmacy all the time, with his friends Ralph and Timmy egging him on. He insisted on going in alone.

"Hi, Mr. Fisher," he said, as he pocketed a small bottle of Evening in Paris perfume. He was in grade four by this time.

"Hello, Pete," said Mr. Fisher, one of the pharmacists.

He didn't call my brother by his nickname; no adults did. They thought it was disgraceful.

"What can I do for you today?"

"Nothing, thanks. I'm just browsing," Pete said.

Sometimes he sat at the counter drinking a chocolate milkshake, thin and frothy, reading Superman comics. Mr. Fisher always gave him the silver container that the milkshake was made in, with the extra bit to top it off. He liked Pete, didn't have a clue about the Evening in Paris or the pen set or whatever contraband he had hidden in his parka pocket. And he didn't seem to mind that my brother returned the comics to the stand, never buying one. Pete did pay for the milkshake, of course, just twenty-five cents in those days.

He wrapped up the perfume—it was close to Christmas—and put it on his teacher's desk. That wasn't even part of the dare. He liked to take things a little further.

His teacher was Miss Pratt, the same one who had turned me in and watched gleefully as I got the strap. No one liked her.

He used one of the tags Nora had bought to attach to Christmas presents. On it he wrote:

in morning light
your eyes are like the sky
from Mr. Dupont

It was his first haiku. No one knew it; not even me.

Mr. Dupont was a grade seven teacher who some of the older girls, including me, had a crush on. He had greasy hair and a lump on his forehead, but his eyes were always half closed and that caused my friends and me to think about how a man might look when he was about to stick it inside you. He made us wonder what that might be like. We did our best to ignore his stringy hair.

I was impressed with Pete when I found out from the kids at school the details of what he had done. Even at his age he knew that Mr. Dupont was the right guy to pick. Miss Pratt had blushed and stuck the package in her purse. There was no way she was going to question it; she was too smart for that.

Pete would do anything. Once during the spring breakup of the Red River, he hopped onto an ice floe and rode it along from the monkey speedway to the old rowing club. A small gang of boys cheered him along. The escapade could so easily have gone wrong.

That type of thing made him exciting to be with. So Pete was a popular boy, in spite of his frailty and his nickname. And his inability to speak to his own sister.

Miss Tufts, the school nurse, caught on to this. She saw most of us at one time or another and she saw a lot of Pete. She must have spoken to him about me and received an unusual response, because she asked to see the two of us together. I turned up, but Pete didn't, so Nurse Tufts called my mother in. Nora must have hated that. She wanted so much to appear normal, even special, in a good way, and the fact that her kids had an unhealthy relationship would have reflected badly on her parenting skills.

Miss Tufts suggested a child psychiatrist named Dr. Bondurant who had an office in the Manitoba Clinic. Nora agreed, of course. Anything for the health and happiness of her children, she said. I sneered inside and even Pete made a face. But we didn't sneer together.

The visits were fun. The doctor saw us both separately and together. When we were together Pete didn't speak. I don't know if he spoke when he was alone with Dr. Bondurant. I'm inclined to think that he did, but I haven't a clue what he might have talked about.

"My brother doesn't like me very much," I blurted out one day when it was just me and the doc. I drew as we talked. He encouraged that.

"Why?" asked Dr. Bondurant.

"I don't know." I lied.

It was drilled into me not to talk about the incident: it was a rule in our house. Pete was not to know of his sister's cruelty. He didn't remember the biting episode, as far as anyone knew; he was only one when it happened. But he wasn't unaware of something dreadful having taken place. He remembered the terror and connected it to me. We all knew it.

"Do you think it might have something to do with your biting him?" Dr. Bondurant asked.

His words stunned me into silence. I worked on my drawing of a beautiful lady with flowing hair; that was my specialty. I used the golden crayon for her hair.

"Your mother told me about it," he said.

"Pete doesn't remember it," I said. "We're not supposed to talk about it."

"It's okay for you and me to discuss it," he said. "Your mother said so."

I found out later that Dr. Bondurant thought the biting incident should be brought into the open, discussed with both Pete and me, but that Nora wouldn't allow it. She made him promise. He was the only one outside of the family at that point, besides my friend Joanne, who knew what I had done.

It puzzled me why Nora had confided in him if she wouldn't let him use it. I came to the conclusion that she wanted him to know that it was my fault and not hers that Pete was weird.

The tiny scar on Pete's face was explained away to the world at large by a fall he'd had at a very young age. The skin taken from his bum wasn't a secret, thanks to me and my big mouth and the constant curiosity about his nickname. Nora hadn't been able to control that part of it.

No one could force Pete to talk to me. Dr. Bondurant tried his best, but Nora thwarted his efforts with her need for secrecy.

Pete still wouldn't look at me either. It was more like he looked through me or at a point just in front of me. There was a hole in my heart on account of it, but I didn't let on. And I didn't want to appear pathetic by loving someone who didn't love me back. So I was inclined to go too far the other way.

Sometimes he bumped into me.

"Watch where you're going, you little simp!" I would shout and Pete would say nothing in return.

One day he drove over my bare foot with his toy fire engine.

"Mu-um!" I shouted. "No Eyes ran over my foot with his stupid toy and it really hurts."

"Why aren't you two playing outside, for heaven's sake? And Cherry! Don't call your brother names!" was all Nora said.

"I don't fucking believe this," I muttered. "The little rat just about ripped my toenail off."

"What did you say?" Nora asked.

"Nothing."

I ran out the back door and over to Joanne's house to tell her that I had successfully said *fuck* in front of my mother.

"Are you sure it was successful?" Joanne asked. "She might kill you when you go home."

We were up in her bedroom, me on the bed, Joanne in front of her mirror, experimenting with the small amount of makeup her mother allowed her to wear.

"Nah, I don't think so," I said. "She can't be bothered with a lot of stuff. She has enough on her plate, she's always saying."

"Well, good then," said Joanne. "Good for you. There's no way I'll ever be able to say it in front of my mum."

"Why would you even want to?" I asked. "Your mum's perfect."

"No, she's not." Joanne blotted her lipstick till it was almost gone, then added gloss.

"Girls!" her mother called up to us. "I've just finished icing some chocolate cupcakes. Would you like to try them?"

"See!" I said.

Joanne smiled. "There's more to her than cupcakes. One time she threw a flower pot across the kitchen."

"Really?"

"Yup. It even had a plant in it."

"Wow! That's great!" I could almost picture it, a girly throw that caused no damage, but a throw, nonetheless.

"Why great?" asked Joanne.

"It just is," I said. "Come on. Let's go eat cupcakes."

We bounded down the stairs. Joanne's lipstick was ruined after her first bite.

Joanne is one of the few friends I've confided in over the years about my relationship with Pete. Oh, I told Henry certain things and one or two other friends heard bits and pieces, but Joanne has always been my one true confidante. I know how lucky I am to have her.

CHAPTER 6

A few days after Stan delivered the journal, I had another go at it. I set myself up with a gin and tonic in my favourite chair in the living room. Over the years I had turned the room into a cozy and comfortable place. Murray smiled at me from his home on the mantel above the fireplace. Spike lay upside down at my feet with his shorts legs pointing upward.

Before I even opened the book, a picture of Nora tapping away on a typewriter at the dining room table flashed before me. There she was, just for a second, in the space between my eyes and the weeping birch outside the front window.

She had wanted to be a writer. The memories welled up: letters to the editor of the *Winnipeg Free Press*, her excitement when one of them was published. It was about stop signs and how there weren't enough of them. She addressed the city planners who made the decisions about where the signs went, letting them know where she felt an extra one or two would be provident.

I remembered the incident that drove her to write that letter. Nora had knocked a pedestrian down with her car because he had ignored a stop sign and she didn't have one. She wanted one so she wouldn't have to drive over people who got in her way. The man wasn't hurt; he even apologized to her. That's the type of thing men did around Nora. But still, it shook her up.

And there were book reviews. She worked like a maniac on those, pencil between her teeth, ashtray full of lipsticked butts. She sent her reviews to the literary page editor hoping he might use one. He never did. And he asked her in a letter to please stop.

She tried our community newspaper next; it was called *The Norwood Press* in those days. But the most she achieved there was a single review of a Harold Robbins book. *Where Love Has Gone*, I think it was. And the editor left out whole paragraphs and changed her sentence structure more than once. She raged.

But kept on. She had an idea for a regular column for housewives. It would contain a review of a book that she had recently read and enjoyed. She would pass her ideas along to women in the hope of expanding their horizons. It was a lie. Nora didn't care about other women and their horizons.

I remembered reading her submission and wondering where she stole the folksy, motherly way of communicating. It had nothing to do with the woman I knew and I was overjoyed when the little paper turned down her idea. They didn't even print the review she had included. This time it was *The Girl Hunters* by Mickey Spillane. The editor explained to her that it wasn't the type of book their readers expected them to review.

If she had a novel in her sweater drawer or a closet full of poems, I didn't know about it. I had never paid much attention to what she did unless it had something to do with me.

Some of her journal entries were written in the voice of a free-spirited woman I never knew, a relative of the one who had tried her hand at a newspaper column, the unknown soul who later sent me letters from the coast:

1974
> *The ducks chatted happily among themselves on the water of Lost Lagoon.*

But more often it was real.

1962
> *The boy scares her. She wonders if a person can be born without a conscience. She thinks she heard that somewhere or read it. Maybe it was in a* Reader's Digest *at the doctor's office.*

Nora had written the genuine parts in the third person. It took me a few pages to catch on to that. The journal was all about her, but her at a distance.

I felt a fleeting connection to my mother: our mutual fear of Pete.

He made a career out of scaring me. One particular instance stands out in my memory.

There was a climbing tree on Lawndale Avenue in the rich guy's front yard, Old Man Whitall's yard. It was a Russian willow. He wouldn't let the kids in the neighbourhood anywhere near it. This made the tree an enticement for all but the most sucked out among us.

We climbed it when his car was gone; we climbed it after dark when we could see him through his front window staring at the flicker of his black and white television set. And the more daring of us, like Pete, climbed it during the daylight hours when Mr. Whitall was at home, even when he was out working in his yard. Once, with rake in hand, he chased Pete all the way to the end of the block, the length of about six houses. No one was hurt and it did nothing to deter my brother.

One hazy afternoon in the summer of 1964, Joanne and I were walking home from the swimming pool. My sandals dangled from my fingers; I was trying to toughen up the bottoms of my feet.

"My mum won't let me buy *A Hard Day's Night*," Joanne said.

"Why not?"

"She thinks two Beatles albums are enough."

"Hmm. That's not good. You have to have them all. Why don't you come over to my house and we can listen to it?"

Nora didn't know what I had or didn't have. It was my babysitting money that I used to buy records. And she was busy with her new job as a secretary and with her boyfriend, Mr. Jones.

We walked by Old Man Whitall's place on the way to our house on Monck.

"There's Ralph and Frankie," said Joanne.

I looked and I saw the two of them, Pete's friends, hiding behind a mock orange shrub at the edge of Mr. Whitall's yard.

The sidewalk was so hot I plunked myself down on the boulevard to put on my sandals.

Joanne screamed and I felt what Murray must have felt before he died. It was like my heart was failing me. I had never heard her scream before.

I looked up at her and then stood to see what she was staring at.

My brother was hanging by his neck from a rope tied to the big tree. His head was awkwardly twisted to one side and as I ran with one shoe on and one shoe off, I saw that my brother's tongue was lolling out of his mouth.

"Pete." The scratchy sound of his name caught in my throat.

I recall the softness of the grass, so luxurious compared to the dry bumpy lawn in our own front yard. Mr. Whitall cared deeply for his grass. But its softness didn't get me there any faster. I ran, but I wasn't going anywhere, like in my dreams of polio. I needed to lift Pete up; that was all I had to do. And he would be okay. Why weren't his friends lifting him up? Why were Ralph and Frankie hiding behind the mock orange?

It turned out I was making some progress after all. I found myself close enough to my brother to see that he was standing on a crate. The crate had been hidden from my eyes by another one of

Mr. Whitall's shrubs, a honeysuckle. I stopped so suddenly that I skidded on the soft grass and the two boys behind the bush burst out laughing. Joanne knew what was going on by now and came to my rescue. Pete did nothing that he wasn't already doing. Nothing had happened as far as he was concerned.

I couldn't quite convince myself that it was okay to leave him like that. Okay, so it was a joke. But what if the crate slipped or Pete went crazy for a second and kicked it out from under himself? So I wouldn't move. Joanne understood; she pointed upward and I followed her gaze from the noose around Pete's neck up the rope to the thick limb above his head. I marvelled at the noose; it was so well done. That was the kind of thing eleven-year-old boys spent their time perfecting while we were imagining what it would be like to kiss John Lennon.

The rope was slung over the limb but it wasn't tied. There was no danger there.

"Come on, Cherry," Joanne said. "Let's get out of here."

"You should be ashamed of yourself, Peter Ring," she added.

He looked at her as if to say, "What's it to ya?" But he didn't speak because I was there.

Joanne left it at that. She didn't want to make anything worse.

I managed to make it out of sight of the boys before I began to cry. Joanne put her arms around me.

"Why do I even care about him?" I wailed. "To him I don't even exist."

"Where did he get such a sick idea?" said Joanne.

"Probably from one of his stupid comic books."

"What's Frankie doing playing with those guys?" Joanne asked. "He's our age."

"And he's usually so nice," I said.

By that time no one called Pete Assface anymore. When he got to be about ten his nickname simply faded away. He grew far too cool for the name to stick.

Joanne and I went to my house. We stretched out on my big old bed and listened to "And I Love Her" and "If I Fell" and "I Should Have Known Better" and it really did make everything okay.

The next day we dressed carefully in our favourite shorts and tops. Joanne's mother packed us a lunch of tomato sandwiches, sliced cantaloupe and Peak Freans and we went downtown to the Metropolitan Theatre where we watched *A Hard Day's Night* three times in a row. That was the first time I tasted cantaloupe; it seemed strange. We almost stayed for a fourth viewing but didn't want to overdo it. After the show, in the early evening, we walked over the two bridges, home to Joanne's house, where I slept over. Her mother had baked cinnamon buns and we ate so many our stomachs hurt and we worried we would be too fat for Paul and John.

I took a break from Nora's journal to freshen up my drink and slip a frozen chicken pot pie into the oven. Spike followed me, his toenails clattering across the floor. He knows if I go into the kitchen chances are good there might be some food involved. He had already eaten his official meal but would have gladly gobbled down another. I gave him a dog biscuit.

The evening sun poured in the living room window. It was hot for early June and I pulled down the blinds to shut out some of the heat. The trees in my yard did a pretty good job of keeping the main floor of the house cool. The upstairs needed air conditioning. I'd had it installed a few years back during a particularly hot summer.

I considered phoning Dougwell Jones on the coast to ask him why he had sent me the journal, but I didn't feel up to it. And really, what difference did it make what his reasons were? I sat back down and read on:

1962

> *Today when the girl asked her a simple question she ignored her completely, acted as though she weren't there. She finds this easy to do. The girl waited a moment or two and then disappeared. The mother will try it more often. (Perhaps it is she who has no conscience).*

A lot of what Nora wrote hit me hard. I remembered her ignoring me, but was shocked by the planning that went into it.

It was in the early days after Pete's first death—which is how I came to think of the fake hanging—that I started up with Henry Ferris. As I remember it, Nora ignored me almost completely that summer when I was fourteen. Henry and I met at the Norwood Community Club, at canteen. That's what the dances were called. He chose me from a clump of awkward girls milling around pretending we didn't care. We danced slowly to "You Don't Own Me" by Lesley Gore. I was terrible at dancing fast so I was glad he picked a slow song. Henry smelled so good that first night. I still don't know if it was cologne or just plain Henry. He was one year ahead of me at school, one year older.

Nora was jealous of our youth, our innocence, of how much fun we had; she was probably jealous of our brand new kisses at the back door. I didn't think about it then, just wondered mildly at her lack of interest, but I know it now. That was why she ignored me to such an extent that summer.

Henry loved The Beatles as much as Joanne and I did. We sang their songs as we walked along the dark back lanes of our neighbourhood. We did the harmonies and Henry talked about starting a band. His parents bought him a guitar for Christmas.

"I'd fuck John Lennon," Henry said.

That didn't seem weird to me at all. "I love you, Henry," I said then.

"Really?"

"Yeah. I love that you'd fuck John Lennon. And that you'd say so out loud."

I also reflected briefly on the possibility of Henry being homosexual, or maybe bisexual, but he wasn't. He just loved John Lennon.

We spent a lot of time necking, standing up at the side door of our house, beside the short driveway that led to the garage. Henry wore glasses. To keep them safe he took them off while we kissed and set them down on the flowerbed next to the shallow step. He wasn't old enough to drive, so when he brought me home we had no proper place to make out, unless Nora wasn't home. Then we went inside and used the living room floor.

There was no decent chesterfield, just the Toronto couch, as Nora called it—slippery, backless and horrible: the place where Murray died. And there was a straight-backed wooden bench that looked as though it was built by someone with no interest in comfort. It was as big as a love seat, big enough for two, but hard and sharp-edged.

"I like it," Henry said. "It looks like it was built by a Quaker or someone." He ran his hand over the upright back. "Fine workmanship."

"It hurts to sit on," I said.

"Yeah. I guess the floor is less painful."

I've wondered about that in the years since—how a couple of parents trying so hard to be normal could have put such a low value on a comfortable place to sit. There were a few other chairs, but nothing good for cozying up in. I'm pretty sure I'm the first generation of Rings or Woodmans to place any priority on physical comfort.

On the nights when we were stuck outside, Henry would reach up and untwist the back door light in its socket, just a little, to give us some privacy while we kissed and touched and pressed up against each other.

"Cherry," he whispered in my ear and reached underneath my top to touch the bare skin of my back.

I wanted to suggest that we go into the backyard and lie down on the grass, but I was afraid he would think I was wanton. Maybe the raw ground was too wild for Henry.

"You're tremendous," he said.

"Thanks." I loved being tremendous.

Before he left he twisted the light back on and retrieved his glasses from in amongst the dahlias. I went inside and tried to act casual in front of Nora, hoping that nothing showed. She paid me no mind. I could have walked in with a miniature version of Henry perched on my shoulder and she wouldn't have noticed.

I never stopped wanting some mothering from her, some advice maybe, on how to live my life, on what not to do, something I could save for later on: don't wear pointy-toed shoes, wash mushrooms really well before eating them, don't say *fuck*, for sure don't say *cunt*.

One spring day, when Henry and I had been together for less than a year, he announced that he and his family were moving away. His dad had been transferred to Markham, Ontario. He was a trainman.

"Don't go, Henry," I said. "I need you to help me keep my life together."

"I have to, Cherry. But I'll be back. And we can write letters!"

He actually sounded excited about writing to me. I couldn't work up any enthusiasm at all. I needed more than words on paper. It was his body and his voice I needed and his soft, soft lips. He probably wouldn't think to say I was tremendous in a letter.

Henry did write to me, long letters about The Beatles, The Kinks, The Rolling Stones, his new school, his new friends; he was sure we could stay together over the miles. He kept assuring me that no one there compared to me. I wrote back, but I wasn't as hopeful as Henry. And I was mad at him for liking his new home.

Nora talked constantly about moving, too, about leaving Murray's ghost behind. I prayed we never would. I didn't want to leave my dad and I thought I might lose him if we left the house, even if we took his ashes with us. And what if I wasn't there when Henry came back?

Murray had left a big life insurance settlement, so Nora didn't have to work to make ends meet. But she updated her skills at Success Commercial College and found a job with another one of her prominent uptown law firms. She wanted to get out of the house.

"This place would smother me otherwise," she said.

I found I spent far more time gazing into my own version of the past than I did actually reading my mother's journal. A half hour could go by before I turned a page. So many memories were flooding back.

After eating my chicken pie I took Spike for a long walk around the neighbourhood. It still wasn't dark when we got home. I had a thought I'd never had before, as far as I could remember. And that was that sometimes in Winnipeg in June the sun shines for a little too long. Sometimes the night closing in is the most welcome part of my day.

CHAPTER 7

I continued to jump around inside Nora's journal; I'm still not sure why. Maybe I had to intersperse the parts that were written before I was born to give myself some breathing room, in case she said something about me I couldn't bear.

Often, though, it was no easier to read about the distant past.

> *Luce lied down for the men tonight. She made me go up to my room before it happened. But when I got up to use the pot I heard animal sounds. I tiptoed to the top of the stairs. Grunts came from the downstairs bedroom. I crept to the landing and snuk a look at the table where they play cards. Jack Logan was missing. I didn't hear Luce make any sound at all but they were doing it to her one by one.*

The only thing that made the reading of this bearable was Nora's tone, the matter-of-factness that she used to cover what surely must have been trembling beneath the surface. Unwittingly, she protected both herself and her future daughter with her abrupt way of putting things. Or, maybe she didn't yet own the words to describe her true feelings; maybe she never would. At this point she still called herself *I*. The references to herself as *she* didn't creep in till a little later. That passage was written in 1939, in the summer, when Nora was just turning eleven.

I was a good five years away from sex when I was eleven. At fifteen I was still a virgin; Henry had been so polite.

A boy named Duane started hanging around me. He was so handsome that I was suspicious of his interest in me. Maybe he sensed my vulnerability after Henry left, saw me as an easy target.

He was a little shorter than Henry, who was over six feet tall. Duane's hair was dark brown and combed back, like a greaser. He wore jeans that were way too tight, but a lot of boys did. My stomach did crazy things when I thought about him or saw him in the flesh.

Duane's family lived just one street over, on Claremont Avenue, but he seemed exotic to me, partly because his last name was different from his sister's. He was a Simkin and his sister, Greta, was a Bower. I liked to think of his mum having had sex with at least two men, probably hordes more. This gave me something in common with him. I had no proof that Nora had slept with anyone other than my dad and Mr. Jones but I had my suspicions.

Greta was my age, but she was one year behind me in school so we didn't know each other well. I couldn't ask her about her brother and trust her not to tell him.

Duane started walking me home from places, like school, the Red Top Drive-In Restaurant, where we hung out at night, or friends' houses, where we went when the parents weren't home.

But I always knew that I wasn't what he really wanted. He never asked me out, never took me to a movie or anywhere at all. Not that Henry had taken me to movies. But at least we'd talked when we walked and he'd taken me to people's houses—not just home from them.

I knew that Duane had done it to lots of girls by then. And for some reason he wanted to do it me.

"Plee-ease, Cherry," he would say when we were necking in various rec rooms around the neighbourhood. "Come on, Cherry. This is killing me," he said. "You're driving me crazy."

I liked that. I liked that I was driving him crazy—if indeed I was—but I wasn't going to let him fuck me. I had learned from somewhere that once you did it, boys lost respect for you and there was no turning back.

The whole winter I turned sixteen, Duane kept at me. He touched my breasts.

"Nice tits," he said and I buried my red face in a pillow so he wouldn't see how he embarrassed me. He touched me over my jeans, gave me my first non-self-induced orgasm that way. He drove me wild, Duane did.

"Nobody kisses me the way you do." He said that to me. Never *I love you*, he didn't say that; I'll hand that to him.

He had plenty of others. I was never his girlfriend. He went steady with girls and kept after me. He took them to parties and movies and school dances; he even gave a girl his ring once. But he kept after me.

I couldn't figure out what exactly I meant to him. He liked me, I guess. We laughed now and then. But why did he invest so much time? Maybe that was it. After a certain point he couldn't give up because too much time and effort had been put in. He couldn't stand that it was for nothing, or for almost nothing.

Henry's letters had fallen off. He still wrote, but not as often and not at length. And he no longer talked about how it would be when he came back. He played guitar and sang in a band and that seemed to be all that was on his mind. They hadn't had any gigs yet, but they had a manager and something was in the works. They called themselves Beaver Tree. It couldn't have been Henry who came up with the name; it didn't sound like him at all.

I talked to Joanne about Duane.

"What am I gonna do?" I said.

"I don't know. I don't think he treats you very well. Maybe it would be best to try and forget about him?"

They weren't the words I wanted to hear. Why couldn't she say that Duane secretly loved me, that she'd heard it from a good source?

"I can't forget about him," I said.

Joanne was in a steady relationship by now with a boy named Quint Castle, who was president of the school. He was a star. Everyone approved and I was jealous till Joanne told me that she didn't love him.

"What?"

"Sometimes I don't even like him," she said. "He's such a know-it-all."

"So what are you doing with him?" I asked.

Quint and I had played together as kids and I did recall him being a bit bossy.

"I don't know," she said. "I've got to get out of it. He kisses like a dead man."

But she didn't get out of it, not for another year. She was in no better position than I was.

My desire for Duane was useless and I knew it. He couldn't give me what I wanted from him, so I began to find it easier to wish for something that was impossible: I wished that I could be him. I tried to see things through his deep brown eyes. This shift in desire undid me.

On a Saturday night in the summer of 1966 Duane got me.

We were at a party at Joe Turner's house. I had gone with Joanne and Quint, had listened to them fight all the way there.

"I don't think we should go to this party," Quint said.

"Why not?" said Joanne.

"There'll be beer and greasers and probably fights later."

"So! It'll be fun!" Joanne skipped ahead and walked backwards for a few steps. "Maybe a beer or two might loosen you up," she muttered as she turned around.

I wished for her words to get swallowed by the windy night, but they didn't. We were between gusts.

"It's not me who needs loosening up, thank you very much," Quint said. "I'm fine just the way I am."

"I'm fine just the way I am," said Joanne.

"Uh-oh," I said.

"Joanne, are you mimicking me?" Quint asked.

"No."

They saw me to the breezeway of Joe's house, made sure I knew some people, and then left. They were too riled up at each other to stay. I heard the snippet, "...kiss like a dead man," shouted in from the boulevard. It was Joanne doing the shouting and I figured that would end it, but it wasn't enough to break them up.

Joe Turner's parents were away. He was one of those guys who was old but still in high school. He hung around with delinquents and it was always a thrill to be at his house. It looked like lots of other parents' houses. There was even plastic on the living room furniture.

But the basement was Joe's world and that's where the party was. It had a bar with a fridge. I helped myself to a beer and sat down at one end of a worn-out couch. I watched Duane come in and notice me while I half-listened to what an older girl named Myrna had to say. It wasn't uninteresting—she was going on about stiffs, as in dead people. Her dad was an undertaker. She seemed to think it was some kind of claim to fame. Maybe it was to some of those people. There was so much I didn't know. But I had trouble concentrating on anything but Duane that night.

There was a room off the rec room that housed the furnace and Joe's weight lifting equipment and a bed. I'd been there before. There were sheets on the bed that smelled like the boys' locker room at school. I knew that because I had been there too.

Joanne and I had snuck in once when our boys had gym. We had gym too, but we told our dim-bulb teacher that our chemistry teacher, Mr. Froese, needed our help with some tricky experiments. It was revolting in the locker room, mostly because of the unholy stink. And we got caught, so it was hardly worth it. We had to apologize to Miss Mott, the gym teacher, and run laps every day after school for one week. Miss Mott got to pick the punishment.

Anyway, that's where Duane led me, away from Myrna and her talk of cadavers, to that stinky grey bed. That's where we did it.

It wasn't that I wanted to; there were other times I wanted him more, like the night when I came through my clothes. But he wore me down; I wore myself down with thoughts of being him.

It hurt at first and then it didn't.

"Does that feel better now?" he asked.

"I guess so," I said.

"How's that?"

"Okay."

It didn't hurt anymore, but it didn't feel good either. It felt like nothing. And I wondered why I had given in. I knew we would never go back to necking now and that was what I loved. That was what I wanted to do for my whole long life. And with him. No one would ever be better than him.

"You've Lost That Lovin' Feeling" was on the record player over and over that night. I never hear that song without the ache that goes along with it.

"I'll go get us a couple of smokes," he said after he had come all over me.

No, don't go. I didn't say it out loud.

I wiped myself off as best I could with a corner of the sheet and pulled my underwear and shorts up over my sticky body. I longed to go for a swim in cool clean water. After five minutes I knew he wasn't coming back. I knew it even before that, but I waited a little longer because I didn't know what to do.

Something—fire maybe—electric fire, licked at the inside of me, pushed its way out through my face, through my eyes. It came close to blinding me as I looked for another way out of the room. There wasn't even a window.

When I opened the door to the rec room no one was looking my way except for a boy alone in a corner by the records: Pete. He had a beer in his hand, one of those stubby bottles that beer came in in those days. He was thirteen years old; what the hell was he doing there? I was almost certain he looked at me that night, through heavy-lidded eyes, although I couldn't prove it. He had a half-smile on his face.

The air in the basement was saturated with smoke and stale beer and sweat.

I ran up the stairs and out the door to the breezeway. It was packed tight with bodies. I closed my eyes and pushed through them to get away. My bed was too good for me that night. I ran to the river.

It was windy but it was a warm wind and I welcomed it against my face. I listened to the laughter coming from the boats moored at the marina across the way. Sleep didn't come but I wasn't expecting it.

When the sky paled in the east I walked home and slipped in the back door, up the stairs to my room. I took off my filthy clothes and lay down on the hard wood floor next to my bed. I covered myself with a sheet and longed for Henry Ferris to come home and save me.

The next afternoon I started my period, so at least I wasn't pregnant. I set out for the Norbridge Pharmacy to get some Tampax. I'd never been able to insert it properly with its stiff cardboard applicator, but I figured for sure I'd be able to get it in now. Maybe I could salvage something from the night before. Usually Joanne came with me to buy my supplies of that sort because it embarrassed me so much, but today I couldn't face Joanne.

As I passed the flood bowl by the community club I saw two boys playing catch in the distance on one of the baseball diamonds. Pete and Duane. I had never seen them together before and thought it must be a mistake. But it wasn't. Against my will I walked closer.

"Go long!" yelled Pete and Duane ran long.

Duane shouted, "Go short!" and they laughed together.

They threw grounders and hit pop flies. They had a bat— Murray's old bat, I guess. They didn't see me. I hid from them before they had a chance.

The idea of braving the drugstore to buy Tampax was suddenly too much for me. My head swam. Seventeen-year-olds don't play with thirteen-year-olds, I thought. I sat by the wading pool and stared at the toddlers till I trusted my legs to get me home.

I didn't tell Joanne what had happened to me the night before. I did mention that I had seen Duane playing with my brother and she agreed that it was odd.

"You should tell your mother," she said. "Duane will be a bad influence on Pete."

"Or the other way around," I said.

Joanne looked at me funny.

I had to tell someone what I had done the previous night so I told a girl named Darlene whom I didn't like very much. I left out the bad parts. She was shocked and made no secret of it. I wished immediately that I hadn't told her.

As the days passed I tried to look on the bright side. I was no longer a virgin and in a way that was a good thing: I had gotten it over with. And it hadn't hurt very much at all. But the overriding feeling was bad. I felt disposable, like garbage, and that stayed with me for a long time. I'm not sure it ever left me completely.

CHAPTER 8

When I tell you about my job and the reason I do it, you'll probably agree with Joanne and Myrna that I'm asking for it, that I deserve whatever I get. Hermione isn't quite so hard on me. She likes what I do, thinks of it as stirring things up which, as far as she's concerned, can never be a bad thing.

It began when I became obsessed with thinking that large parts of the history I read are either lies or mistakes, that the way people want to be remembered and the prejudices of those keeping the records skewer the facts. We get the odd pocket of truth, but generally it comes out wrong.

And then there are the silences in the history books—the childhoods, the friendships, the family fights. Where were the home lives—the parts that shaped those who were written about? Elusive long-dead truths raise my curiosity but leave me edgy because I can't know them.

I decided to try to add something genuine to the history being written today. I did this by interviewing people and asking them questions they couldn't answer with clichés or platitudes:

When was the last time you cried? I asked.

Describe to me a time you recall in your life when you really hated someone.

I don't believe you, I often said.

When did you last feel afraid, sad, hopeless, happy, proud, lustful? Describe those occasions.

Have you ever hit someone? No, but really.

Have you ever taunted someone?

Were you made fun of as a kid? What for? What did you do about it?

Have you ever planned your own death? your own escape? someone else's death?

Those were the types of questions I asked.

The *Winnipeg Free Press* published several of these interviews and after a few years I was lucky enough to get a regular gig with the paper.

Public figures were my favourite subjects. And writers and teachers and business people and religious leaders and advocates for the downtrodden. If their answers didn't ring true I threw the interview away. I spoke to them face to face—never on the phone. I wanted to see their eyes.

Pissing people off was part of it. I'd had more than one death threat.

Myrna thought I was wasting all my years of education. We bickered about this but I had no argument for her other than it was what I wanted to be doing. I wanted to tell the truth. Besides, she didn't need a science degree for what she was doing, running the family funeral business, so what was she doing criticizing me?

The work wasn't always satisfying. Sometimes weeks would go by without my getting anything real. The paper was very good about my column appearing sporadically. I was paid by the interview. But I tried to keep it regular, as best I could.

My column was called *No, But Really.*

I have a small income as a result of Murray's life insurance policy. If I live frugally, which I do, I can get by.

Joanne never bothers encouraging me to move up in the world; she's known me for too long. But other people sometimes say things like, "Dr. Ring, is it? My goodness, you could be..."

Yeah. So what.

When I got something good for a column—like when a woman who makes her living being poor and droning on about it suddenly blurts out that she would like to slap some of the poor people she knows, hard across the face, it feels good.

I guess I am asking for it: to be exposed, embarrassed, killed. But other than the odd letter of attack on me to the editor of the paper and those death threats I mentioned, I haven't been tested. I'm almost certain I feel ready to take what anyone is going to give me, but I could be mistaken.

Joanne thinks it's just a matter of time till someone shoots me. She's probably right. She has a theory that I crave punishment. Maybe she's right about that too.

CHAPTER 9

I've mentioned Myrna now, more than once, so I should explain her presence in my life.

When I was sixteen I got my first job. I worked at The Bay in the men's shoe department. In those days men's shoes were serious business and I had to take a course, on two Saturday mornings.

There were several of us starting at once and we learned terms like *last*, which we had never associated with shoes before. I forget now what it means but I do recall that it was the most important thing to remember about shoes, according to our instructor. His name was Ken McLeod and he was the manager of the men's shoe department.

In order to work, I needed a social insurance number, and to get one of those I needed my birth certificate. So I enlisted Nora's help. She dug it out from somewhere after my asking her for it on four consecutive days.

I studied it, this flimsy record of my birth, and was shocked to see the date written as November 13, 1949.

Nora was sitting at the kitchen table, smoking and flipping through a copy of *Ladies' Home Journal.*

"It says here I was born on November thirteenth," I said.

She looked at me with a blank expression fixed around the fag between her lips.

"I thought my birthday was on November fourteenth," I said. "That's when we've always celebrated it."

If you could call Nora's pitiful icingless cakes a celebration. Sometimes there was a present; sometimes there wasn't.

"Let me see that," she said, snatching the worn paper from my hand. It tore along one of the thin creases. "Well, what do you know!" She laughed.

I noticed that her teeth were yellowing and I rejoiced in her misfortune.

"Imagine us having it wrong all these years," she said.

"It makes me feel kinda funny," I said.

"Why?" Nora asked. "It had a hell of a lot more to do with me than it did with you. I did all the work and it was no picnic, believe me. Not like with Pete; he just slid out like a slippery eel."

I took the paper back and folded it carefully. Maybe I could get a new sturdier one when I applied for my social insurance card.

A heaviness in my stomach dragged me down so far I had to lie on my bed for a while; I'm not sure of the exact reason, whether it was the incorrect date or the fact that Nora didn't think my birthday had much to do with me. Both, I guess.

Anyway, the birth certificate got me my social insurance card and I worked Saturdays at The Bay through most of grade twelve, some Thursday and Friday evenings as well.

I hated it. I dreaded busy days but slow ones were worse. We weren't allowed to sit down when there were no customers and sometimes I wanted to scream out loud. Maybe that's where my hatred of standing up began. I like walking, I love walking, but I hate standing for more than a couple of minutes, like at bus stops without benches.

The only part I liked about working at The Bay was the time I spent in the employees' lounge, smoking enthusiastically. I knew it was smoking that had turned Nora's teeth yellow but I also knew it would never happen to me.

It was there that I ran into Myrna again, the undertaker's daughter. She was a Norwood girl, but two years older than me, so we hadn't had much to do with each other till then. By this time I was fascinated by her situation. Her huge house on the other side of St. Mary's Road was attached to a funeral parlour. The place where she ate, slept and bathed was home to dead people, with their blank eyes and their various stages of decay. Stiffs, as she still called them, got worked on there, laid out by her father and his helpers. For all I knew Myrna was one of those helpers.

"Myrna, dear, hand me that tube, would ya," her father might say. "Stick it in this corpse's neck, please, and we'll drain all his blood out before embalming him."

"Sure thing, Pop," she would answer.

I was afraid to ask her questions about the business even though I longed to hear her talk about it. Sometimes I could have sworn the stink of formaldehyde was on her. It might have been my imagination but at the time I didn't think so.

Myrna attended university and worked only weekends, the same as I did. She worked in the girls' clothes department, which seemed a much better deal. Both of us got a ten per cent discount on all of our purchases. She helped me pick out clothes that suited me. I was grateful for this because I didn't have a clue. For instance, I loved pink. Myrna convinced me that I looked like an idiot in pink, a deranged bunny rabbit was how she put it, and that greens and rusty colours suited me better.

I had been a little nervous about approaching her in the lounge because she was older and all, but she soon came up to me and it didn't take long before we were making fun of people together and laughing a lot. Once we started talking she told me that she was going into the family business but that her parents insisted on a university education first. They also insisted on the job at The Bay in the hope that it would improve her people skills.

"Do you want to go into the family business," I asked, "or are your parents making you?"

"I want to," she said. "My sister doesn't. She wants to get as far away from it as she can. But I like it. Especially when no one else is around, when my dad's not there talking too loud. It can be so quiet and...I don't know...awe-inspiring? I feel at home with the dead."

She smiled and I liked her very much at that moment.

Myrna could be nasty, even back then. I found it a relief to have a nasty friend, someone worse than me. I could picture her biting a baby.

She actually played tricks on people. There was a woman in her department named Muriel whom she played tricks on all the time. Poor Muriel was in her forties, skinny and lonesome. The Bay was her life, according to Myrna.

"Hey Muriel, what's shakin'?" Myrna would call across the lounge as Muriel walked in.

Muriel grimaced into her shoulder and took a seat as far away from us as possible.

"Last Friday night I really got her going," Myrna said.

"What did you do?"

"I phoned her at home and disguised my voice and asked her if Moses was there."

"Moses?"

"Yeah."

"What did she say?"

"Nothing much. Just that there was no Moses there, that I should double-check the number. She didn't seem to think it was weird that someone these days would be named Moses."

"There are Moseses," I said.

Myrna squinted at me with a look that said I didn't have any more of a clue than Muriel. She lit up another cigarette from the one she had just finished. If we smoked fast we could squeeze two into our break.

"Okay, so then what?" I asked.

"I called her back and said, 'May I please speak to Lucifer?' Muriel said 'Who?' Then I said, 'Lucifer. You know, Satan? I need to speak to him.'"

I laughed.

"She asked if it was me. 'Is that you, Myrna?'" Myrna said, in imitation of Muriel who sat across the room from us staring straight ahead. "I guess I didn't do that great a job of disguising my voice."

"Or you're the only person she knows who would phone her and say such things."

"She called me evil, said it'll all come back to me one day."

"It might," I said. "I'm not sure if anyone is off the hook if they're intentionally mean."

Myrna looked at me as if I were speaking a foreign language, Russian maybe, one of the hard ones.

She didn't give a hoot about a lot of things and I think that's what drew me to her. But she also scared me. What if she used one of her nasty ideas on me one day? What if it involved a dead person? After I began to understand the reverence she felt towards the dead I stopped worrying about that. But still, I kept my fascination with her family's business to myself. I was afraid she would invite me over to look at corpses, to share the experience, and I knew I would take her up on it against my will.

Her cavalier talk about stiffs was all for show. She was like Nora in that way, careful about what she put out front. But she had cracks that you could slip through, unlike my mother, who lived behind a wall of stone.

One Saturday in the spring of 1967 Myrna came home from work with me. She backcombed my hair and put eye makeup on me and I looked like someone I had never met. We went to a dance in Windsor Park at Winakwa Community Club. We had to take a bus to get there. I knew as soon as we arrived that I was in over my head. Myrna got swept away soon after we arrived.

Joe Turner was there; he was the only person I recognized at first.

Boys approached me because they didn't know who I was and because I didn't look like me. I looked like someone who, at the very least, would give them a hand job.

I went to the restroom and washed the makeup off my face. Then I brushed my hair till the backcombing was out.

There were lewd messages written all over the walls in pen, in pencil, in lipstick. Some were carved into the old wood:

ROXIE SUCKS COCK

EAT ME NICKY, PLEEEESE!

Some weren't so lewd:

PANTS VS TROUSERS VS SLACKS

Those last words cheered me up; I laughed out loud.

When I found Myrna she was dancing with a guy who had both hands on her bum. The song was "Somethin' Stupid," by Frank and Nancy Sinatra.

"I'm leaving," I said.

"Party pooper," Myrna said. "What happened to your face?"

The boy turned around and I saw that it was Duane. He had a black eye.

"What did you do to your hair?" Myrna asked.

Duane looked through me; it was as though he'd taken lessons from Pete. Or maybe he genuinely didn't recognize me: his least memorable sexual experience.

I was well over any feelings of desire for Duane, but I wasn't over what he'd done to me. That stuck like rubber cement.

Last I heard, which wasn't long ago, he was in prison in Quebec. Armed robbery, I think it was. So Duane's not doing well.

Joe Turner gave me a ride home that night and he didn't even ask me for a hand job. I guess he thought I was just a kid, without the big hair and eyeliner.

I didn't hate Myrna after that night. But it took me quite a long time to want to hang around with her again. A person could disappear if left in her hands, fall into a hole somewhere when no one was looking, where no one even knew there was a hole.

She pursued me quite fervently; I still don't know why. We never had much in common except that for some reason we liked each other.

Myrna and Nora liked each other too. That really got to me. It was one of the main things about Myrna that drove me crazy. It seemed peculiar to me that a kid would want to hang around with the mother of another kid. Not just peculiar. Wrong. One time she dropped in on me when I wasn't home. She used to do that—drop in. I didn't like it; I preferred some kind of plan.

It was late in the summer, the final week before university classes began. When I arrived I found her and Nora sitting on chairs in the backyard. Mr. Jones had bought two wooden lawn chairs for us. The grade eight boys in shops class at Hugh John Macdonald had built them. They were a lot more comfortable than the nylon ones Nora had brought home from Canadian Tire. Mr. Jones had painted the new chairs green.

Nora and Myrna were facing each other and one of Nora's feet rested on Myrna's bare knees. My friend was painting my mother's toenails.

"What the hell is going on here?" I asked and they both looked up at me.

The nail polish was pearly peach.

"Myrna's helping me get ready for the party," Nora said.

She and Mr. Jones were going to a party at the Castles' place, Quint's parents' place. They lived in a huge house by the river.

I turned around and went inside the house. I felt sick to my stomach. As I hurled up my Red Top cheeseburger into the toilet I could hear the sounds of giggling wafting up from the backyard, through the bathroom window.

Myrna also developed an interest in Pete as time went by and he was no longer a kid. She asked me about him all the time.

He was handsome in a pale poetic way, smart in school, and good at sports. Not football, he was too slight for that, but he played on the basketball team and with his agility he beat the high school's all-time record for leaping hurdles.

And Pete had a way with words. None of them were ever directed my way, but whenever an occasion called for a poem, the high school principal, Mr. Longbottom, would ask Pete to write a haiku. Here's an example:

pigskin champs
lead the parade
autumn rains down

That was when the Norwood Broncs won the football championship. Pete's haiku were often related to sports, as that was what was most often celebrated at our school.

I don't know if they were any good; I've never been a studier of poetry. It was just amazing to me that he did it. I saved them, the ones I knew about, the ones I liked. They seemed to me like they came from a good part of Pete, maybe the best part.

Here's another one:

pageantry in snow
players are the figures
in a dream

That was after some kids from the school enacted the nativity scene at an outdoor Christmas festival.

Mr. Longbottom hung Pete's haiku up on the bulletin board next to photos of the occasions that they described. He had the art teacher, Miss Kirby, write them out in fancy lettering.

I developed a renewed interest in being friends with Pete. It was the haiku, I think, that sucked me in. I made a few tentative gestures. I asked him some questions, which I hadn't done for years, about his poems, about his hurdles, about his clothes.

"You seem to prefer wearing your shirts tucked in," I said cheerily.

That one was more a comment than a question.

I left long spaces of time between my efforts, not wanting to cause a disruption. But I never got an answer.

When I baked a blueberry pie I took him a piece on a plate and placed it next to him on the front steps. Later, when he was gone, I picked it up and offered it to a neighbour kid who was riding by on his trike. I sat with him while he ate it, watched his face and hands turn blue. Then I fetched a damp washcloth and we cleaned him up before he pedalled off home.

The girls at school were infatuated with Pete and he counted several of them among his friends. But he didn't have a real girlfriend till the summer he was sixteen. I heard him say to someone that he had observed the way girlfriends could take the wind out of your sails. His choice for his first girlfriend remains a puzzle to me to this day.

It wasn't Myrna, but not for want of her trying. She was cute in a short, cheerleader kind of way and she had a trace of wildness in her character that I fully expected would appeal to Pete. But he remained aloof from her, maybe because she was my friend, maybe because of the huge age difference between them, although I couldn't imagine that mattering to him. Here was his chance to get laid, for Christ's sake. Even when she used her trump card—access to the dead—he resisted.

She invited me over in a loud voice when she knew he was in the next room.

"There's a guy at the funeral home who blew his brains out in a car. Do you want to come and look at him?"

"No," I said. "But thanks for asking."

We did go to the Red Top Carwash where we heard that the car, a '57 Caddy, was being cleaned. Pete was there, too, with Tim and Ralph, gaping, like we were. A man took a hose to the inside of the car. Something slippery and grey spilled out onto the pavement. I'll never forget the smell. It reminded me of worms on sidewalks after rain.

"What if I'd said yes?" I asked Myrna.

We sat in a booth at the Red Top with our root beers and our cigarettes. The restaurant was next door to the car wash. The same three men owned both businesses.

"Pardon?" said Myrna.

"What if I had said yes, I did want to see the dead guy?"

"I knew you wouldn't."

"But what if I did?"

"I wouldn't let you. It's private."

"So it's all for show, you and your fancy offers."

Myrna smiled. "Don't tell anybody."

I woke up screaming that night. Nora's boyfriend, Mr. Jones, came to check on me. He stood in the doorway of my room and asked if everything was all right.

"Yes, thanks," I said.

What else could I say to a stranger?

CHAPTER 10

I wanted to set Nora's journal aside for a while after reading the bit about Luce lying down for the men. But I couldn't leave it for long. It was like a drug, one of the nasty ones, that whispers your name like an angel and then leaves you feeling wretched before you're even done with it.

So I sat down again with a glass of iced tea and read on.

August, 1939

> *Luce locked me in the root seller before the men came. The men and Darcy. When I started out yelling Luce said she'd stuff my mouth with dirty rags to shut me up so I didn't yell for long. I did nothing wrong I swear. I reckon it's to do with the men having at her but that's nothing to do with me. It's not fair. She stared down at me with her bad black eyes, the sky white behind her all wrong. I thought skies were sposed to be blue.*

I took Spike for a walk, to get us both some air. We went to the river. Spike wanted to go in the water, but I didn't let him. It's full of poisons.

We walked down Taché Avenue to Norwood United Church and on to my friend Hermione's place, Cuts Only. She was still open. Hermione is a haircutter who does me when I need it and Joanne and Myrna too.

"Well, well, well," she said as we scrabbled through the door. Spike slipped on the wooden floor in his excitement to get to her. All conceivable colours of hair stuck to his fur. Hermione was cutting her own hair, taking long hanks of her salt and pepper tresses and snipping them off near her scalp.

She put down her scissors and scooped Spike up in her arms. She kissed him and he sneezed and licked her face and sneezed again.

"What on earth are you doing?" I asked.

She laughed. "I'm going to shave my head. Hey! You can help!" She set Spike down and he shook himself off as best he could and sat blinking up at her.

"Why?"

"I don't like the white mixed in with the dark brown. It makes me look dowdy."

"No, it doesn't."

"Yes, it does." She looked in the mirror. Half her head was short tufts, the other half long and wavy. "Maybe when it's all gone white I'll be okay with it."

"Are you sure about this?" I asked.

"Yes, I am."

"How about just colouring it or highlighting it or something?"

"I don't do colours. I don't do highlights. That's why this place is called Cuts Only. You know that."

"You could make an exception for yourself," I said.

Hermione filled a bowl with water and stray hair and set it on the floor for Spike, who slurped eagerly till he had his fill. Then he coughed for a while and Hemione went back to her image in the mirror.

"I've been reading Nora's journal," I said and sat down in her second chair to watch.

"No wonder you look as if someone knocked you on the head with a shovel."

"It's hard to read, but I have to do it."

"I know you do, hon."

"Tell me again why I have to do it?"

"Because you want to find out what made Nora tick."

"Oh, yeah."

After she had finished cutting her hair Hermione got out her shaving equipment. "Okay, this is the part where you help me."

By the time we were finished, her beautifully shaped head was bare and smooth and her eyes looked enormous.

"You actually look quite nice," I said.

Hermione laughed. "It would take a hell of a lot more than a haircut to destroy these looks, babe."

I laughed too.

"Let's drink," she said.

"Yes, let's."

Hermione poured bourbon into two glasses and we sipped and talked for a half hour or so about the possibilities for tomato sauces. Everyone in our cooking class was taking a turn concocting a sauce and then presenting it with a small amount of pasta for the rest of us to taste. I dreaded my turn. I pictured noses turning up and comments like, what the hell went into this mess?

The door opened and Hermione's last customer of the day walked in.

"Well, look at you!" he said.

The new look suited her and she has kept it to this day. She still plans to let it grow when it turns completely white.

She went back to work and I headed home with Spike leading the way.

I cooked some spaghetti, did a pretty good job of getting it al dente, and stirred it up with butter and salt and pepper. That's the way I like it best. Sometimes I mix a little olive oil in with the butter but today I couldn't be bothered. I'm really not much of a cook.

It was eight o'clock by the time I finished eating, too late to go back to the journal if I was going to stick to my plan of not reading it late in the day. But it turned out I wasn't sticking to that plan. Maybe it was Hermione's bourbon that caused me to throw caution to the wind and sit down with it again. Just one more passage:

> *She gave me a blanket and a pillow but it was cold down there with the jars and the potatoes. I fell asleep before the men went home but the cold woke me twice. Also, when something crawled across my neck I woke to hear them still at it. It was morning before she came to get me. The stink of Darcy Root was on her. I've seen boys in the fields with sheep. I see what they do to the ewes. But Darcy is a girl too. I don't know what she does to Luce. Something. That's for sure.*

Aunt Luce was saving Nora from a nightmare of larger proportions than her most frightening stay in the root cellar but my mother didn't see it yet.

I let Spike out for a last scramble around the yard and then headed up to bed with a Robert Parker book. I needed to laugh.

CHAPTER 11

To think that it was only ten years between the summer that Nora smelled the stink of Darcy Root on her aunt and 1949 when I was born. This was my mother who was holed up with spiders on the dirt floor of a pitch-black root cellar.

I know she was sent into the city after Luce died. It must have been soon after that summer of '39 because I believe she was just twelve when Mr. Trent had the sense to get rid of her.

What a handful she must have been for her foster parents—the Kennaughs, they were called—with her messy past and her rough country edges. A major project for them, for sure, and for her teachers. She was a success story though, if immaculate grammar and self-presentation to the outside world were the yardsticks.

Maybe it had been a source of pride for Nora that I went to university. This had never occurred to me before. I attended the University of Winnipeg.

Henry Ferris turned up in my second year Twentieth Century History class. His dad had been transferred again. We got back together, but it felt different this time. I wasn't as interested in kissing him, not like I had been before my Duane experience, but I stuck it out because his friendship was important to me and I didn't want to lose that. It seemed complicated and unfair, my merely moderate physical desire for Henry: one of life's bummers. I struggled with it; I didn't want to feel dishonest, but the spark was missing.

"You've changed somehow," Henry said.

It was a windy fall day in 1968. We were sitting on the lawn in the quadrangle at the university. "Helter Skelter" was blaring out of a window in the men's residence. The Manson Family hadn't done their killing yet.

"Sorry," I said.

I smoked and Henry studied me.

"No, it's not bad or anything," he said. "You just seem a little further away or something, sort of...secretive."

"Sorry."

"No, it's okay, Cherry. It's nothing you have to apologize for."

That was all he said. He never pestered me about anything.

"Henry?" I put my cigarette out in the grass.

"Yes."

"If we were ever to split up, you would never tell anyone all the secrets I've told you, would you?"

"God! Of course not!"

"Like stuff about Pete and everything."

By this time I had told Henry everything about biting Pete, about our visits to Dr. Bondurant, and some parts about the state of our relationship. I wanted him in the picture and besides, he saw a lot of it for himself.

"Cherry, no! I would never, ever say anything to anyone."

He had risen to his knees and he took both my hands in his. He didn't argue with me about the splitting up part. Maybe he sensed that we were doomed.

Henry was in a local band by now. It didn't take long for him to hook up with a ready-made group. Everyone needed a singer and Henry was good; he was often compared to Stevie Winwood. They even changed the band's name from Prairie Lightning to O Henry. I disagreed with the change; it made them sound like bubble gummers, but I kept my mouth shut. Henry liked having his name up front like that. So far, they had played one school dance and a fashion show. Their dream was to play in pubs.

It was odd, because everyone wanted to sleep with band members—it was a fact of life—but during that particular time, he seemed too familiar to me, and too good. I wanted guys with their own apartments downtown, places that stank of dope and sweat, guys who ignored me if I said it hurt. Henry still lived with his parents and cared too much about pleasing me.

Nora's man had been around for several years by then. His name was Dougwell Jones and he wore a hat when he was out and around. It was an old-fashioned hat like the one Humphrey Bogart wore in *The Maltese Falcon*. My dad had worn hats like that a long time ago. Mr. Jones seemed to me like a throwback. Maybe Nora was searching for her past, for the days before Pete and me, but after her move to the city, that slim period of time when she still had a chance.

Mr. Jones taught science at the same school where Murray had been a teacher. Nora had known him before Murray died. I found that part of it distasteful. As though she had been lusting after Mr. Jones when my dad was still alive.

I chose not to know him. He interfered with my memories of Murray. He appeared around corners when I least expected to see a grown man and I couldn't get over my disappointment in who he was, or wasn't. I didn't go as far as to pull a Pete on him, but I just gave him the basics in terms of greetings and answering the odd question. That is one of my regrets: I wasted a fine presence for many years.

Mr. Jones and his first wife hadn't been able to have any children. I wonder sometimes if he had hoped to be a father of sorts to Pete and me. Neither of us gave him much of a chance.

One day, not that long ago, maybe eleven years or so, I was sitting in one of Hermione's chairs getting a trim. It was soon after I discovered her. It came out somehow that Dougwell Jones had taught her when she was in grade eight. She had lived in the inner city as a kid and gone to Hugh John for junior high. She was too young to have been in one of Murray's classes but she remembered Mr. Jones. He was her all-time favourite teacher.

I remembered the pictures of Murray's classes and had no trouble placing Hermione there with the young ruffians and the wayward girls.

"Man, I can't believe you're practically related to Mr. Jones," she had said that day. "Does he ever come to visit you?"

"No. He lives on the coast with my mother," I said. "And I'm pretty estranged from her."

"I understand what that's like," said Hermione. "My mother's dead, thank God."

We laughed.

"Mr. Jones convinced me that I was smart enough to go to university," Hermione said. "I had been getting all set to take the commercial course, you know, typing, Gestetner machines and all that. But he talked me into taking the university entrance course."

"What's a Gestetner machine?"

Hermione laughed. "I don't know."

"Did you go to university?"

"No. But I could have."

"Well, when I get talking to Dougwell again I'll tell him about you and how you're getting along."

"Yes. Do. Tell him I'm the best fuckin' haircutter in Manitoba."

Sometimes I think that Dougwell's goodness entered me through osmosis. I couldn't keep him out entirely. He had a grace about him that touched the core of me and I feel that would have sat well with Murray.

He pretty much lived with us by the summer of 1969. He was addicted to Nora, as I think Murray had been. I don't know how else to explain it. She had something that both men wanted, that neither man wanted to live without. It was more than sex. The thing she possessed mingled with a certain energy inside both of them to create the powerful mists that ensnared them. It is the only way I can visualize it and the only way I can keep from laying blame. Oh sure, Nora tried to be sexy and she worked to keep her figure and all, but the thing that captured them wasn't something she had control over; it just was.

And that co-mingling of magical mists was what was missing between Henry and me. From where I stood, anyway.

CHAPTER 12

That summer of '69 my brother got his driver's licence. He was sixteen and I was nineteen, getting ready for my third year of studies at the university. Pete would be entering grade twelve at Nelson McIntyre Collegiate.

Sometimes Nora lent him her car to run errands for her or to go out with his friends if he promised not to drink or carry on. Her car at that time was a 1966 Chevy Malibu.

"If I find out you've been drinking and driving my car, I'll have your balls in a vise," she said to Pete more than once.

She had a way of putting things that made my body shrink up into itself. I don't know what her words did to Pete. Nothing, to all outward appearances; they looked to breeze right by him and his lazy smile. He reminded me of a silvery Airstream trailer with its hard surface and smooth shoulders, gliding down a shimmering highway to its end and on. Most things slipped off those shoulders.

Pete loved driving Nora's Malibu and he made sure she never caught him drinking.

"When I drink, I drive more slowly," he said.

I heard him explain this to Henry, who was waiting for me at the kitchen table. It was an August evening and we were going out to see *Midnight Cowboy*.

"It balances out with my slower reaction time," Pete said.

"Hmm," said Henry.

Pete was more of a doper than a drinker, anyway, and Nora hadn't caught on to drugs yet. We were all sure that smoking pot turned you into a better driver, or a more cautious one, at least. And Pete was a lucky guy; everyone said so.

Later that same night Henry and I were kissing at the back door pretty much as usual. He had twisted the light off and as I remember it, he was flailing about to an unprecedented degree. My heart wasn't in it.

"Your breasts are tremendous," he said.

Henry still said "tremendous." It irritated me that he used the same descriptive words as he had used years before. Couldn't he come up with something new?

He undid my cutoffs. I did them up again. He undid them once more. And I did them up again.

Pete was out in Nora's car. He most likely hadn't been drinking or smoking dope because the damage he did as he swerved into the driveway required a normal to fast speed.

We didn't hear him coming. I do remember hearing Thunderclap Newman singing "Something in the Air," a song about callin' out the instigators and haulin' out the ammo. It must have been playing on the car radio when the front end of the Malibu slammed into me.

Pete, of course, didn't see me.

He stayed behind the wheel of the car staring straight ahead. Someone was in the passenger seat; it was his girlfriend, Eileen, but I didn't know it at the time. The headlights were on.

Henry wasn't hit. He held me in his arms and said, "Keep still, Cherry. You're going to be okay."

I didn't feel a thing.

Eileen's screams brought Nora and Dougwell running. And then I passed out for the most part; I was in and out. I recall the ambulance attendant telling me in an irritable voice to stop pushing. That confused me because I hadn't realized I was doing anything at all.

It turned out I needed a new hip as a result of the accident. My right hip was ruined. I was one of the first people to undergo that operation at the St. Boniface Hospital.

But it was the back door light being out that was the part of the event that Nora wanted to dwell on. That way she could blame me.

I stared at her in disbelief from my hospital bed. Dougwell stood silent. I wondered why he was there. How could he stand her? My theory about his attraction to her hadn't yet been formed at this stage.

My body ached and I shook with anger.

"Have you even spoken to Assface about his part in all this?" I asked.

It had been years since I had called Pete by his old name. I'd outgrown it. I hated that I used it now.

"He didn't see you," Nora looked to her man for help.

Dougwell shifted from one foot to the other.

I liked him very much for not speaking right then.

"The bulb was unscrewed in the bulb hole," Nora said.

"He didn't see me because he chose not to," I said. "Sister? Duh. What sister?"

Nora sighed and walked over to the window. She lit a cigarette (you could smoke everywhere in those days) and gazed out, probably wishing she could leave the mess of her family behind.

"Isn't it time that my punishment ended?" I said.

She didn't turn around.

"Punishment?" Dougwell asked. "Punishment for what?" He looked from one of us to the other.

I don't know why I was so sure Nora would have told him what I had done to Pete when I was four years old. As I watched a delicate blush creep up the side of her neck I realized that, of course, she was too ashamed to tell even him about what her daughter had done. It would reflect on her.

What I wanted to do then was blurt it all out. But when Nora turned her eyes from their place in the distance to my face, I changed my mind. There was always darkness in her eyes; it never went away. But at that moment it turned black and it hurt my new hip to keep looking at her.

How had she explained Pete's behaviour toward me all these years? Maybe Dougwell wasn't curious. Some people aren't. No, that wasn't it. Nora would have written it off to a typical rivalry between a brother and sister, glossed it over and then gotten snappish when he pressed her for more. That was the way she would have done it.

Things changed between Pete and me after the accident. That's what everyone called it: an accident. I called it attempted murder, but only to myself. And only some of the time. I couldn't make up my mind. I vacillated between certainty that he had tried to kill me and belief that it was an accident. I think I know the answer to that now, but I still have doubts in the middle of the night when I lurch awake in my sweat-drenched bed.

Pete came to see me in the hospital where I spent fourteen days. And he did see me, for what appeared to be the first time, or the first time since he was one year old, anyway. He still didn't speak, but he looked—man, did he look. Shyly, at first. At least, I took it for shyness; I don't know what the hell it really was.

I said, "It's okay, Pete. Look at me long and hard if you want. I don't mind."

And I didn't. So he sat in a hospital chair when no one else was visiting, or even if they were, sometimes, and stared at me. Stared till he must have known the sight of me as well as anyone could know it, as well as Henry. He had to know every freckle on my smooth nineteen-year-old face, every nuance of colour in my auburn hair, looking at me like that.

Sometimes Eileen came with him. I didn't like my brother's girlfriend. She was short and chunky, with a wide mouth and teeth so tiny they looked like baby teeth. They didn't go with her mouth at all.

Eileen was in training to be a practical nurse and I guess she figured this was a chance for some hands-on practice. She bustled around my hospital room, plumping my pillows, freshening my water, discussing me with anyone who happened in.

"I think Cherry has more colour in her cheeks today," she said to a nurse I'd never seen before. "Don't you?"

The nurse smiled at me, and I smiled back, conspiratorially, I hoped.

Eileen even called me *dear*.

Once, when I sighed, she said, "What is it, dear?"

"It's that I want to go to sleep," I said.

"Oh. Well."

I closed my eyes and she took the hint and shuffled off, after whispering loudly to Pete. He stayed on to look at me some more.

It puzzled me that she was his girlfriend. He could have done much better. Myrna would have been better, although I wouldn't have liked it. Maybe Eileen gave good blow jobs. Her teeth certainly wouldn't get in the way.

On the sixth day of my hospital stay, an orderly helped me to stand up. I was a little woozy, but the dizziness passed quickly. On the seventh day, the same orderly wheeled me to the physiotherapy department where I took a few steps with the help of parallel bars. Soon I graduated to crutches. I practised in the hall outside my room. Before long I was confident enough to enter other halls and travel to other floors.

Pete accompanied me on these walks, taking in my height, which was tall for a girl—five feet, eight inches—and my slim shape beneath the thin hospital garb. I was a little self-conscious as I watched him looking at my breasts and long legs, but I figured it was important for him to do it, so I genuinely didn't mind. My brother was seeing me for the first time. I really believed that.

If Henry or Joanne or Myrna dropped by, Pete would fade into the background while we visited but his eyes never left me. Joanne thought it was creepy, Myrna thought it was sexy and Henry thought it was interesting.

The nurses marvelled at Pete's attention to me, telling me how lucky I was to have such a brother. They didn't hesitate to allow me to leave the floor because they knew I was in such good hands. They didn't have a clue.

A couple of times I tried to get him to talk, just a hello or how are you doing, but that wasn't going to happen. Not yet, anyway. I thanked him once for being there and a look of puzzlement flashed on his face and was gone. No one was more puzzled than I was.

Dougwell was excited about this breakthrough behaviour on Pete's part. He thought we were all going to live happily ever after.

I was grateful to him in a guarded sort of way. It was as though I was seeing him for the first time. He played Murray's part; my dad would have been ecstatic by the new development.

Nora remained cool. It would have taken a lot more than Pete seeing me to fire her up.

CHAPTER 13

I didn't return to university in the autumn after the accident. Physically, I could have. The crutches were a snap—I could dance with the crutches. But I didn't feel like it; I wanted a break, some time off—to get used to my new hip and, bigger than that, the fact that Pete could see me. And I needed time to listen to *Abbey Road*.

My decision worried the hell out of Nora. She was concerned that if I took time away I'd never go back. That's what had happened to Donna Wright from over on Birchdale Avenue. She had been so smart in school.

"And look at her now," Nora said. "She's twenty-five years old and a cashier at the Dominion store."

It was a warm Saturday in September and we were in the backyard, in an area Nora referred to as the patio. It was a slab of cement with clover growing through the cracks. Nora and I sat on the wooden chairs that Dougwell had brought home; he sat on one of Nora's nylon ones. He looked horribly uncomfortable.

"There is something to be said for getting your schooling when you're young," Dougwell added. "It gets harder and harder to go back."

Nora must have talked him into taking part in this conversation. It wasn't like him to offer me advice.

"Remember how hard it was for your dad?" Nora said.

When Pete and I were small, Murray had taken university courses at night to finish up his education degree.

"And I'm paying for your education now," Nora added. She lit a du Maurier with a gigantic table lighter shaped like a swan. "You might not be so lucky when you're Donna Wright's age. Anything could happen."

"Like what?" I said.

Nora sighed and two streams of smoke escaped her nostrils.

She looked like a dragon, a beautiful, worn-out dragon-lady. For the first time I noticed the vertical lines around her lips. She couldn't like those.

I looked at Dougwell, who was staring at her. Maybe he was noticing the same things as I was.

"Like, we may decide we have better things to spend your father's hard-earned money on," Nora said.

"It wasn't hard-earned," I said. "It's a life insurance policy. What could be more easily earned?" I apologized to my dad in my head for being such a jerk. Tears welled up in my eyes.

"He had to die for us to get that money," Nora said. "I'd say that's a pretty steep price to pay."

Dougwell stood up and walked over to the hose reel by the garage. The hose was uncoiled and he began the noisy job of winding it up. It was a homemade contraption that Murray had built and no one ever thought to give it a lube job.

I was ashamed of both my mother and myself.

Nora got up and went in the house. I sat and watched Dougwell struggle with the hose. He went inside the garage and came out with a can of oil which he squirted into the joints of Murray's makeshift rack. It helped. By the time he was done a quiet creaking sound was all the noise it made.

"Way to be, Dougwell!" I wanted him to know I didn't blame him for anything.

He smiled at me.

I sailed down to the river on my crutches and found a bench to sit on. I wore long skirts that fall while getting used to my new hip. Joanne made two of them for me; she's always been a good sewer, just like her mother.

The smell of sugar beets was in the air. When I made my way home I saw Pete and Eileen getting into Nora's car in front of our house. Eileen saw me and waved. She touched Pete's arm and he turned around to look. I stopped mid-stride so I could wave at him without losing a crutch, but he didn't wave back. I flushed with embarrassment as though I had been picked last for the baseball team.

"Prick," I said quietly.

"Asshole!" I screamed after the car as they pulled slowly away. How could he not wave back after staring at me for weeks? He owed me way more than waves. How in the fuck could he not wave back?

When I got to the house Dougwell made me a grilled cheese sandwich and sat with me in the backyard while I ate it. I think he knew I was upset and he wanted to help me without prying.

We were alone. Nora had gone over to Norwood United Church to help with a rummage sale. Dougwell told me about his wife, Barbara. It was the first time I'd heard anyone talk about her.

"We were planning a Central American holiday when Barbara's illness began to get the better of her," Dougwell said.

"I'm sorry."

From the way he spoke, quietly and constantly glancing over his shoulder, I knew he was telling me something that Nora didn't want me to know: Barbara wasn't dead yet.

Or as Dougwell put it, "She lives in one of the municipal hospitals in Riverview."

Everyone knew what that meant. You were never going to get out; you were a goner.

He thought I should know.

It wasn't long after Barbara had been hospitalized that Dougwell bumped into Nora at the Safeway. He had met her before at school functions when she was with Murray. He had admired her, he told me, and blushed. So I knew he meant her appearance, maybe her full breasts and her sultry air.

"Nora's so different from Barbara," he said. "She scares me a little." He chuckled. "But that's okay. It keeps me on my toes." He ran his hand over the new paint job on the arm of his chair. "Barbara never frightened me at all."

I wondered afterwards if he felt he'd said too much. It was as close as Dougwell ever came to me in those years, but it was through no fault of his. And I know it would have been different if he hadn't moved away.

CHAPTER 14

C herry Ring needs work. I don't mean a job. I mean that my being, my self, needs work done on it to make it right and sound, like a dilapidated house or a broken-down car.

I'll try to illustrate the type of person I became by telling you more about my job at the *Free Press*. One of the first interviews I did was with Dr. Bondurant, the psychiatrist Pete and I had seen when we were kids. He never stopped wanting to help me. We met in one of the snack bars at the Health Sciences Centre and this is how it went:

C.R.: Dr. Bondurant, what led you to become a psychiatrist for children?

Dr. B.: Well, I've always gotten along with kids. I like 'em. And I figure if people are troubled at such an early age, there may be hope for them. It may be possible to help them turn something around.

C.R. So are you saying that by the time people become adults it's too late for psychiatry to be of any help to them? I snickered here. *Some of your colleagues might take issue with that.*

Dr. B.: No, I'm not saying that. At least, I don't think I am. I just mean that the earlier you tackle a problem, the more likely you are to solve it.

C.R.: Uh-huh.

Often I paused for long moments. That gave people a chance to dig little holes for themselves if they weren't comfortable with the silence, or if they felt the ball was in their court like Dr. Bondurant did now.

Dr. B.: I'm sure my able colleagues in the field of adult psychiatry accomplish a great deal of positive work.

C.R.: Isn't psychiatry mostly just about dispensing drugs?

Dr. B.: It's true, drugs often play a large part in treatment. There are some wonderful drugs available these days that help to make difficult lives much more bearable.

I'm on one of those drugs myself, which Dr. Bondurant knew, but he wouldn't have mentioned it under threat of death. He did, however, look at me as though I had bitten him hard on the nose.

C.R.: Is it true that some psychiatrists use only drugs as treatment? They don't spend any time talking to their patients, trying to get to the root of their problems?

Dr. B.: Yes. That's true.

C.R.: Do you ever do that? Use the drugs-only method?

Dr. B.: No. I generally try to talk to the kids, get them to open up to me.

C.R.: So you've never done that? Not once?

Dr. B.: Well, maybe once or twice. When it seemed the only way.

C.R.: Drugs as the only way for kids. That doesn't bode very well for the great long future ahead of them, does it?

Dr. B.: No, it doesn't.

He patiently stuck it out as I went at him, Dr. Bondurant, who had been nothing but good and kind to me. I battered him terribly.

My columns hurt people. I told the truth at the expense of feelings. But people want to be thought of as truthful so they seldom refused to be interviewed. They even invited me to do them.

I still read history books; I can't help myself. Sometimes I fill in the blanks or change things to the way I figure it would have been. I spend a lot of time on these projects—rewriting books—and again, certain of my friends think I'm wasting my time. But I enjoy it and that's worth something.

Who is the bigger failure, Nora or me? As I put this to paper I find I don't know the answer to that.

The more I read of her journal the less inclined I felt to work on my column. I had set up an interview for a Wednesday afternoon in mid-July with Mitch Podolak, the founder of the Winnipeg Folk Festival. I'd met Mitch before and liked him. I wasn't entirely sure if I would be up to my usual methods and even if I was, I could picture him flattening me instead of the other way around.

So I phoned on the afternoon before the interview and cancelled. He laughed and tried to set up another time. I hemmed and hawed and he laughed some more.

"Are you chickening out?" he asked.

"Maybe."

We left it that I'd call him in the fall when "things had settled down."

"What things?" he asked. "What settled down?"

"I'll talk to you in the fall, Mitch," I said and hung up.

He may have still been talking when I put the phone down, but I was seriously unable to continue the conversation.

I poured myself a gin and tonic and sat down with the journal.

September, 1939

> *The men were coming for cards. I hid in the barn so Luce couldn't find me. Then I listened from under the porch to the talking that went on. Where's the littlen? Darcy Root said. It was quiet for a minute before Luce said asleep. That littlen looks about ready for pluckin, you ask me Darcy said. Nobody asked you. That's Mr. Dickson Trent talking now. He laughed, though, and that made him sound like he was on Miss Root's side. You'll just have to do with me. That's Luce. I barely heard that last part. It was like she was talking into her sleeve.*

My mother, the littlen. I shivered in the heat.

The ice cubes had melted in my drink and Spike was asleep upside down at my feet when I closed Nora's journal for another day.

CHAPTER 15

Nora was cool toward Henry for a while after the car accident. I guess she figured she was supposed to be upset about him undoing a light bulb and kissing her daughter passionately. But it was just an act, like her flower garden and her church circle. And it didn't last long. He was impossible not to like, with his polite ways and his ability to talk to parents. Once he showed up at the door with chocolate on his chin and Nora actually hugged him, something she never did to Pete or me. She'd had several rye and Cokes, but still.

Henry and I fizzled out. We didn't even make it till Christmas. It was my fault; I didn't have any energy for him. And the university and the gigs where O Henry played were bursting with young women who did. We said goodbye in early December and wouldn't see each other again for a couple of years. It was Henry's idea to cut off all contact. He didn't think he could be just friends, which was what I suggested. I could have slit my own throat for saying it; if a man ever said that to me I'd slit his for sure.

I missed him for a long time, but I didn't give in to the urge to get in touch. I didn't even go to see O Henry play in the pub at the St. Vital Hotel. I missed some great nights from all accounts, but it wouldn't have been fair to him, the state I was in. Henry deserved better. I felt chill and hard inside, like I imagined Nora to be. He needed someone soft and warm.

The winter was cold. All winters are cold in Winnipeg but the year of my new hip seemed brutal. I felt drafts in the old house that I'd never noticed before and I wore socks to bed for the first time in my life. I had graduated to a cane before the snow fell and could walk with no support by the end of November. But sometimes I used my cane anyway, after new snow fell and the sidewalks were extra slippery or if I had to take a bus. It kept people from banging into me and was something solid to hang on to.

Pete drank a lot that winter, eased up on the dope and got into rye whiskey like our mother. I heard him early on Sunday mornings, vomiting in the bathroom. And later in the day, he whispered into the phone.

"What happened last night?" he would say, talking to one of his friends. He groaned. "Do you think I have to phone anyone to apologize for anything?"

And sometimes he'd make more calls, full of excuses and apologies.

"I'm sorry I pulled the chair out from under you."

"I feel terrible about making fun of your hair."

"I'm so sorry I left you at the social. I sure hope you managed to get a ride home. It was cold last night."

That time he was talking to Eileen. Her knee froze on her walk home from the Elks Hall that January night in 1970. She had worn only pantyhose under her short dress and coat, never dreaming she would be left to walk home. They split up after that frigid winter night. The knee that froze was vulnerable for her whole long life after that and she never stopped blaming Pete. Or loving him: he was her only love. She said as much to me, not so long ago.

Pete was kicked off the basketball team for missing too many practices. Nora didn't find out till the playoffs when she and Dougwell were all set to go and watch him do his stuff.

My brother and I didn't get any further. His staring at me stopped seeming like a positive thing. It got tiresome, then creepy, like Joanne thought it was from the start, and finally I had to start yelling, "Quit staring at me!"

He listened to what I said, if someone else was around. I could tell. But if it was just the two of us, he paid my words no mind. So I stayed out of his way, backed way off. I had nothing left to offer him. Maybe my basket of offerings wasn't very full to begin with but I didn't know how to change that. It wasn't that I didn't care. But I didn't have it in me to push. I came to think of him as the mad woman in the attic, except he walked among us and was a boy.

I spent a lot of time in my room over the winter, listening to *Abbey Road* and *Cheap Thrills*, smoking a lot of cigarettes and a little bit of hash. The dope helped me to be nice to Nora. She was oblivious to what I was doing, just noticed if I was grumpy or pleasant.

"You're awfully easy to get along with lately," she said once when I had made my way, heavy-lidded and thirsty, downstairs to have a look in the fridge. She smiled at me.

I felt confused and shuffled back upstairs with just a glass of water. Was it me and the way I was that kept her from smiling at me like that more often? Could she and I have something more if I changed? Was it more than just her fault?

When I ran out of hash I didn't buy any more for a long time. That little encounter with Nora freaked me out. I was more comfortable being crabby and unhelpful.

In the spring I took a job in the office at the Dominion store. I filed and typed and dealt with complaints. My hip still ached. The manager's idea was that when I improved physically I would head out onto the floor as a cashier. My idea was that I would quit in a year or so and go back to university with the help of Murray's life insurance money.

Dougwell was okay with this. He was an optimist, like Murray.

He sang the Dominion's theme song, that one about why more Canadians shop at Dominion than any other store. Apparently it was mainly because of the meat.

I sang along with him and we laughed. Later, when he was puttering around in the yard, I heard him whistling the tune and I felt a huge fondness for him. I wondered again how he could stand my mum.

Nora was sullen. She was tired of me. I think she thought I would never be gone. I would live with them forever, the pathetic daughter who never managed to break away.

When she was my age she had been on her own for four years. She took the commercial course at school and landed a job as a secretary the Monday after she graduated. It was the first job she applied for, I remember her saying, more than once. Soon after that she moved away from the Kennaughs into her own apartment. She left them behind.

Once, when she was more talkative than usual, I asked her why she hadn't kept in touch with the Kennaughs. After all, they had been her family for four years.

"They were paid to be my family," she said. "You would have to pay me to go back to see them."

"Didn't you like them?" I asked.

"They were all right. They were an improvement over what I came from."

I think Nora missed Henry more than I did. She saw his leaving as a door closing. My mother didn't like me very much. Ever. I try not to dwell on it.

CHAPTER 16

I was stretched out in the hammock in my backyard. It was hung between two trees, an ash and an oak. Joanne sat on a lawn chair close by, one of Dougwell's old wooden ones. It needed a coat of paint.

"Let's take kick-boxing lessons," she said.

"Kick-boxing?"

"Yeah. I'd like to have a sport that I'm good at."

"We walk our dogs," I said.

"Walking our dogs isn't a sport."

Spike had heard the word walk twice and he was up on his feet, on full alert.

"But kick-boxing? Why not yoga, something more leisurely?"

Joanne and her husband Grant had moved back to Norwood when their last kid left home and their house in Southdale grew too big. We had stayed in touch over the years but it was so much better now that she lived only two streets away.

"My hip couldn't handle it," I went on.

"Oh," Joanne said. "I forgot about your hip."

"I'm on the list for a new one."

"Really?"

"Yeah. This one is a little outdated; it's a one size fits all."

"You're kidding!"

"No," I said. "They build much better appliances these days, more personalized. That's what they call them: appliances."

"Well, good then. When's this going to happen?"

"I don't know. I'm on a list."

Joanne was eating salted peanuts in the shell and was covered in peanut dust. I was eating sunflower seeds, spitting the shells over the side of the hammock onto the lawn. Spike had sat down again and was gnawing on a piece of rawhide.

"My new hip will be titanium," I said.

Joanne let out a low whistle.

We both love salty snacks. If I were to interview myself I would say that munching on popcorn with my head on a pillow, staring through the leaves of an oak tree is one of my favourite things to do.

Blue and green are my favourite colours. I think it's because of the times I have spent all my life, staring through many shades of green at the deep blue Winnipeg sky.

There are other things I like: throwing a stick for Spike, reading history books, playing Scrabble with Joanne. She always wins and I'm a poor sport, but she doesn't mind it when I call her a slippery slapper.

Sometimes four of us play: Joanne, Myrna, Hermione and me. We drink wine and swear a lot, call each other cunts and cocksuckers. In the summer we play outside. We shout so loud we wake the neighbours. We eat snacks and smoke.

But that day in late July it was just Joanne and me and by the time the sun got lost behind the oak tree we decided on yoga at the Norwood Community Club. There was a class coming up in the fall. My Italian cooking class had finished at the end of June. It was amazing how little I had learned. Maybe I would do better with the yoga.

When Joanne left I went in the house. I remembered some focaccia that I had made at my cooking class and I took it out of the freezer. I ran a bath and immersed myself in eucalyptus-scented bubbles. Before I even soaped myself up there was a loud commotion outside so I got up to look out the bathroom window. It was a Green Guy deweeding my lawn. *Green Guys* is a lawn care outfit that I hired to contaminate my little patch of the universe. I got a special deal because I planned a year ahead. I closed the window to keep out the toxic fumes. My guilt was strong enough that I knew this was the last time ever for the poison. I returned to my bath, which had suddenly lost its appeal. It was just another chore.

Afterwards I threw on a sundress and sat down at the dining room table with a glass of iced tea and a slice of the focaccia. Nora's green book sat on the table in front of me. Several days had gone by since I read about "the littlen" being ready for plucking and I hadn't picked it up again.

Sometimes I was afraid that her words would bury me. Like quicksand they would suck me down, fill my lungs and close in over my head. But I was determined not to let that happen, always taking the time to digest each entry before I went on to the next. Digest and then what: blow out or assimilate? I didn't know, still don't. Some parts will be with me always. I do know that.

My Italian bread wasn't very good. Maybe I shouldn't have frozen it. I chewed slowly for a while and then gave up and threw the rest away.

I reopened Nora's journal.

1939 Fall

> *Luce has quit eating. She cooks for Mr. Trent and me but she doesn't eat anything herself. I asked her about it and she said she eats when I am at school. She's lying.*

Uh-oh, I thought, and closed the book.

CHAPTER 17

I t was late on a warm cloudy afternoon. Rain was in the forecast. July makes me even lazier than usual. I have never stopped thinking of July and August as the holidays. I looked out the upstairs hall window and saw that Joanne was in my hammock. I hadn't noticed her arrival.

"Beer?" I called out the kitchen window.

"Yes, please," she said.

Her dog, Wilson, was snorfling around the edges of the yard. I let Spike out first and Wilson was in ecstasy. She is a huge mutt who thinks Spike is king. He appears to only tolerate her, but I'm quite sure she means more to him than he lets on. Wilson bounded over to me when I came outside with my arms full of beer and pistachio nuts. There were bits of twigs and old leaves attached to her coat.

"Grant's got that weed-eater thing going," Joanne said, "so I had to get out of there."

"Tell him I can hear it all the way over here," I said.

"Can you?"

"No. But tell him that."

"It's the loudest noise I've ever heard next to his leaf blower," Joanne said. "I can't believe he thinks it's a good idea."

"What day is it?" I said.

"Friday."

"Let's play Scrabble."

"Should we phone Myrna and Herm?" Joanne said.

"Yes."

"We can order pizza or Chinese food."

"Or Vietnamese," I said. "This'll be great."

"You make truth seem evil, Cherry," Myrna said later. "You make it seem wrong. Your column should be called *Dr. Cheryl Ring is Evil.*"

I chuckled when Myrna said that, but no one else did. I cared what she thought. It wasn't the first time she'd mentioned my column but it was the first time from that particular angle. She had a few drinks inside of her.

We had decided on Trivial Pursuit and we were sitting around my dining room table: Myrna, Joanne, Hermione and me. Smoking is allowed, as is swearing and drinking too much.

Three of us have the odd toke if Hermione brings something. She's the only one of us who goes to the effort of buying it. There are no teenagers or husbands to worry about at my house, just Spike, the silken little lout. And he enjoys our company if we don't get too raucous.

Dope is out of the question for Myrna. She hasn't done anything but alcohol and cigarettes since 1975, when, after dropping a tab of Windowpane acid, she received a call from her dad who tracked her down at a party to tell her that her mum was dead,. Just exactly what you don't want to happen. It was sudden too, a blood clot in the brain. It went downhill from there. Myrna got it into her head that she was supposed to "do" her mum. She ended up in the mortuary mucking about with the equipment, poking around at a dead woman who wasn't her mother, thinking she was "the warm-up act," as she put it, until her younger sister found her and took her in hand. Nightmare city.

Myrna looks pretty much the same as she did twenty years ago, just a little heavier in the face and thicker through the middle. She isn't fat, but she no longer goes in at the waist, so she looks a bit like a fire hydrant, being so short. Plus, she wears red all the time.

"What smash 1971 tune ran eight minutes and twenty-seven seconds?" asked Hermione.

We were playing the Baby Boomer Edition.

"'American Pie,'" I said.

Joanne and I were partners.

"Good one," said Herm. She's the best sport of all of us.

Joanne rolled again.

"Obsession with the truth can be as harmful as obsession with anything else," said Myrna. "Your column could be called *Dr. Cheryl Ring's Dangerous Obsession.*"

Her words were scaring me, but I didn't want her to stop.

"Hmm," I said.

"Too much truth isn't always a good thing," she went on. She poured herself another glass of red wine, spilling a little on the game board and on her shirt.

I went to the kitchen for a damp cloth and dabbed at our sticky and faded board. I could hear thunder rumbling in the distance. Rain began splatting against the window in huge drops.

"Sometimes," Myrna said, "in certain circumstances, a lie is a good thing."

"I don't agree," I said and tossed the rag toward the kitchen. It hit the doorjamb and landed on the floor. Spike went and sat beside it.

"How was torturing your good friend Dr. Bondurant beneficial in any way?"

"That was ages ago," I said.

"So!"

"It wasn't torture for him. He could take it."

"Bullshit!"

"Plus, I think it benefitted the ratio of truth to lies floating around in the stratosphere. That needs evening out sometimes."

"That's horseshit," she said.

I knew it was. I considered telling her she looked like a fire hydrant.

"You don't care about people," Myrna said.

"That's not true," I said. "I care about you guys."

"Do you?" she said.

"Okay, for a pie," Herm said. "Whose last big hit was 1963's 'Forget Him'?"

"Bobby Rydell," said Joanne. "Yay! We got a pie! *Forget him, 'cause he ca-an't see-ee you*," she sang. "*Forget him 'cause he has no eye-ey-ey-ey-eyes.*"

Hermione laughed. "Those aren't the words, you crazy old slut." She gave Joanne a little shove.

"God, we're good," I said. "No one's better than us."

"I'm not old," said Joanne. "You're old."

She got up and looked out the dining room window at the rain. It was coming down in torrents.

"Do you, Cher?" Myrna was still at me. "Do you care about us?"

She hadn't called me Cher in a long time. I didn't like it. She pronounced it *chair*, just so you know. She was drinking fast and her words were starting to come out flabby.

"Yes! How could you not know that?" I said. "And don't call me Chair. I don't like having a name that sounds like something you sit on."

"Would you tear me to shreds if you interviewed me for your column?" she asked.

Myrna was a lousy drunk.

"I wouldn't interview you," I said.

"Why not?"

"Because I wouldn't want to hurt you."

"But I'm an undertaker. You could crucify me if you wanted to. You could accuse me of all kinds of weird things."

"I wouldn't want to." I knew where this was leading.

"That in itself is dishonest then, isn't it? Keeping certain people safe from your toxic pen because you think they are your friends? You're a liar, Cherry, the biggest liar of them all."

"Okay, Myrna. That's enough," Herm said. "I'm going to take you home before you make me slap you."

"Yeah, I should call it a night too," Joanne said from the window seat. "I want the rain to stop," she went on, pressing her nose against the glass. "I hate the rain."

"How can you hate the rain?" Hermione asked, joining her at the window. "It's one of the good things."

"I worry about our roof leaking and seepage in the basement, and mould forming in the closets. Our house is so old."

"Do you have any of those things?" I asked. My house was older than Joanne's.

"No." she said. "And I'm worried that I'll get wet and never get dry again."

"Maybe you should see a psychiatrist," said Myrna.

She rested her face on the table now. I wanted to tousle her curly hair but I was afraid to.

"The rain's gonna let up tonight. It's starting to right now," said Herm. "Look. It's coming down lighter. And the thunder's getting further away. Tomorrow's going to be sunny and dry. It's going up to twenty-six." Hermione always knows the forecast.

She assured Joanne and me that she would drive Myrna home. Myrna had gone quiet and I decided not to say anything more to her, but I felt terrible.

Joanne stayed with me after the others had gone. I put Van Morrison on the CD player. *Poetic Champions Compose.*

"Are you okay?" I said after Joanne was settled into my best chair with Spike in her arms. "Since when do you hate rain?"

"I don't, usually. I think Myrna got me down. I hate it when she gets drunk and horrible."

"You think she's right about my column, don't you?"

"Mm-hmm," said Joanne.

"Do you think she's importantly right?"

"What do you mean?"

"Do you think what I do matters enough to be important in a negative sense?"

"Yes."

I opened a window and lit a cigarette. The cool damp air sucked the smoke outside.

"It hurts you to get to people's truths if you have to harbour so much hate to do it. And I think you do."

"You think I harbour hate?"

"Yes. And you feed it and nurture it. I'm surprised it hasn't burnt you down to a little pile of ashes."

I shivered and closed the window.

"To say nothing of the other people you hurt with your so-called truths, like poor old Dr. Bondurant. Jesus, I can't get over that you did him. I think the benefit of truth to lies that you talk about floating around out there is less powerful than hateful vibes that come out in bits of cruelty. They cancel out good stuff all over the place."

I looked at Joanne, at her clear brown eyes and her thick mop of white hair.

She carefully set Spike down on the floor, stood up and found her umbrella by the front door. "I gotta go," she said.

I followed her to the door. "I'll think about what you said."

"No, you won't." She kissed me on the forehead.

"Yes, I will."

Spike rolled over on his back at Joanne's feet so she would give his tummy a rub before she left.

"See you tomorrow," she said to us both.

She had a short walk home to their bungalow on Ferndale Avenue.

I stretched out on the couch in the living room to listen to the rest of the disc. The couch is one I bought from The Bay soon after my family went away in 1971. Spike lay across my chest and I drifted off during "Alan Watts Blues." I didn't wake up till early morning when Darius Widener's weed-eater accompanied by his dog Mitzi's barking frightened me into an upright position.

CHAPTER 18

Nora and Dougwell Jones were together for years before they finally married. Mr. Jones' first wife, Barbara, had had a series of strokes and was in the hospital, the Princess Elizabeth, I think. She wouldn't die. Dougwell must have hoped she would and for sure Nora would have wished for her death, but Barbara Jones hung on till December of 1970 when one last stroke finally did her in.

Nora married Dougwell five minutes later.

It was possible that they sensed disapproval in the community or maybe they felt guilty all on their own. Whatever the reason, they decided a change of scene was a good idea and made plans to head for the west coast. Jobs were easy to come by in those days.

The idea was to take Pete with them and leave me behind. More precisely, I refused to go. I had Joanne and Myrna and my job at the Dominion store. And there was the house on Monck Avenue and a whole lot more. Henry was back in the city, though I never saw him. Winnipeg was where I wanted to be; I thought it was the centre of the universe.

It all felt good to me. It would be a chance to dwell less on my crippled little family. I needed distance from my mother and my brother, some good long Canadian miles stretching out between us.

Pete was as excited as I've ever seen him. Vancouver, man. He had never been anywhere. He had friends who worked on the trains in the summer and they came back from the coast with tales of pure drugs and easy girls. The way he saw it, the time was right for a move to Vancouver. He had taken two years to finish grade twelve at Nelson Mac, had taken the two-year plan, as he called it. So he was between things when they left. There was talk of his going to Simon Fraser or UBC or maybe going to forest ranger school. This was all from Nora. If Pete had any ideas about his future he kept them to himself.

My mother wanted to sell the house but I dug in my heels and promised to keep it up. At her expense, of course. Murray's expense.

"It's a good investment," I said.

Dougwell agreed.

She liked that. It was the right thing for me to say. And she was okay about giving me an allowance as long as I took the upkeep of the house seriously and promised to return to school in the fall. It was worth it to her to have me out of her hair.

I worried about Murray's ashes; I didn't want Nora to take them. My concern was unnecessary, although I kept a vigilant eye out till the three of them were packed up and ready to go. The urn stayed in its box in the closet along with the picture of Murray that Nora had taken down from the mantel when she first brought Dougwell home.

They left on the hottest day of the summer in 1971.

The flat dry world lost its colours in the midday heat. Nora was a drab cardboard cutout in the front seat of Dougwell's Buick 6. She smoked and tapped her fingernails against the outside of the passenger door. The red of her nails was the only colour in the day.

Dougwell fussed with tarp straps—several suitcases were fastened on the roof of the car—and Pete leaned against an elm tree on the boulevard, waiting for the last minute before getting in. His oily blond hair fell past his shoulder blades. I thought I caught a whiff of his unwashed body but it could have been my imagination, like with Myrna and her embalming fluid. Joanne insisted she couldn't smell anything on Myrna.

I didn't know what to do, how to handle this strange goodbye. So I did nothing. Pete also did nothing; Nora reached out a hand to me, but retracted it as I began to move forward. Dougwell came around the car and gave me a one-armed hug.

"You can change your mind any time and join us," he said.

"Thanks, Dougwell," I said, knowing there was no chance.

The car was idling now. It had the strangest sounding engine I ever heard. I couldn't imagine it completing the trip to the coast, but it did.

Pete got in the back seat and rolled down the window. I thought he winked at me, but I could have been mistaken about that, too.

I looked away and saw Joanne walking towards me with the Avery family dog, Boo, at her side. She still lived at home with her folks. I was so glad to see them. I wished they had been there in time for Pete's wink. Joanne would have been able to tell me if it had happened or not; I hoped it hadn't.

They drove away and *The Beverley Hillbillies'* theme song ran through my head as I waved goodbye to the flapping tarpaulin.

The bleached-out stop sign at the end of the block did nothing to stop the car; it drove clear through. The pale day swallowed my family; they were gone.

"I wonder if I'll ever see any of them again," I said.

We sat on the front steps with Boo a short distance away on the grass. He was an elderly dog who liked to sit back a bit so he could keep his eye on the whole picture, the whole herd, which in this case was just Joanne and me.

"Of course you will," said my stout-hearted friend.

"It's funny." I said. "Of the three of them I'll miss Dougwell the most. We were just kind of getting started."

Joanne threw a tennis ball for Boo and he stumbled to his feet.

I didn't say it out loud, but I wasn't sure I ever wanted to see Nora again. As it turned out, I didn't.

CHAPTER 19

Nora continued to surprise me with the words in her journal. I found myself leaving her distant past and leaping ahead to the second last entry. It was written early on in the Vancouver years.

1972 winter
> *If only it was the girl here with her on this dreary coast. And the boy the one she left behind. He has grown so morose. At least the girl made her laugh.*

I didn't know what to do with this information.

"When did I ever make my mother laugh?" I asked Spike.

He stood up and went into the kitchen. I heard a cupboard door close. That is what he often does when his suppertime is drawing near. He gently closes any open doors with his nose.

It wasn't quite time. I stared into space and thought about the past.

One of the first things I did after my family left for the coast was put Murray's picture back on the mantel. He looked so young. I remembered thinking that in not too many more years I would be as old as my dad was when he died. Then I would be older than he ever was. I left his ashes in the closet, but I didn't forget about them, as Nora surely did.

A letter came to me now and then with a return address from North Vancouver. The Nora who wrote letters was not my mother. The way I finally figured it was, she was writing to someone else in her mind. If she had been writing to me she wouldn't have used phrases like "majestic mountains," "gay old time," and worst of all, "silly me." She came across like Anne of Green Gables or maybe Emily of New Moon writing home to a simple friend.

Dougwell sometimes added a line or two at the bottom, often encouraging me to come for a visit.

They seldom mentioned Pete. There was one line about him having a little trouble finding his niche—this from Dougwell—and an ecstatic note from Nora saying he was working part time at the post office for Christmas. Part time is good, she wrote, because it leaves him time for his poetry. She was sure he was the next Leonard Cohen. This infuriated me for some reason. I loved Leonard Cohen; I didn't want Nora smearing him with Pete dirt.

It was hard thinking up topics when I wrote back, so mostly I just talked about school and the house and Joanne. And Henry, how we were together again.

I hate to compare Henry to a pair of comfortable shoes, but that's how it was. He pursued me again and the fit was just so good. Even sex was easy with Henry and he was technically very able. I had to pretend he was someone else sometimes, but often just his being Henry was enough. I didn't mention those sorts of things in the letters, just that we were together again and some of the things we did: movies, concerts, Henry's gigs.

There was a dog in my life by then, so I wrote about him and how great he was. He was a beagle named Diesel. I had never had a pet before because of Pete's allergies. Plus, Nora hated dogs; she was afraid of them.

I was back in university, as planned. As long as I stayed in school, Murray's money kept coming. That was the deal and it was okay with me. I liked school. By 1973 I had an honours degree in history and I was working on my master's.

Less than a year after Nora wrote that puzzling entry about my making her laugh she called. It was a gray afternoon in November. She rarely phoned, so I knew something was up.

"Pete hanged himself," she said. "He's dead."

"Oh Lord." I pictured his distorted face hovering beneath the branches of Mr. Whitall's willow tree. "Are you sure?" I asked. My heart pounded in my ears.

"Of course I'm sure. It was that masturbatory thing boys do, you know, that sexual gratification thing. It went wrong."

"So it was an accident."

"Yes. But it's not necessary for anyone but the family to know the details."

Of course, more secrets.

My first thought had been suicide. I didn't know about the thing that Nora was talking about. And I didn't want her to explain it to me. I hated what she was saying and the way she was saying it.

"When?" I asked.

My cold blood was turning my brain to ice. I stared out the dining room window and watched two sparrows find disappointment at the empty bird feeder.

"Sunday night."

Today was Wednesday.

"Sunday night? And you didn't let me know till now? My brother is dead and you don't tell me till now?"

I knew not to expect much from Nora, but this was insane. My brother had been dead for days and I hadn't known.

"Aren't you even sad?" I wailed into the phone.

Nora was quiet.

"Cherry? Dougwell here. Your mother's pretty upset."

She had handed me off.

"Why didn't you phone me sooner?" I asked.

"I thought it was up to your mother," he said. "I didn't want to butt in."

"Jesus," I said. "Should I come?" I didn't want to go, but who was looking after Pete, after his arrangements?

"I don't think it's necessary, unless you want to," said Dougwell.

"What about the funeral and everything?" I asked.

"We've had Pete cremated. Nora doesn't want a service."

Pete was gone.

"May I speak to my mother again, please?"

When Nora was back on the line I asked, "How could you have let all this happen without letting me know?"

"We're letting you know now," she said. "It hasn't been easy on us either, Cherry."

"Why wasn't there a service of some kind?" I asked.

"I didn't feel up to it," Nora said.

"People never feel up to funerals," I went on, conscious of my voice rising. "They have them anyway. It's what people do. Why do we have to be so different from everyone else in the universe?"

I wanted my dad's arms around me now more than anything. More than Henry.

"Dougwell has been a tower of strength," Nora said. "I was the one who found Pete. He was still alive. I tried to lift him up and cut him down to get some breath back into him, but it was too late. I watched him die. It was a horrible death."

I remembered running toward Pete, across Mr. Whitall's lawn, running to lift him up. But I felt no sympathy for my mother. She didn't love Pete; she didn't love anyone. She was only telling me this to make her own part in his death more dramatic.

"Thank you very much," I said. I didn't want to hear any more from Nora. The grieving mother bit made me nauseous; she hadn't practised enough for it to ring true. Even from Dougwell it would have been better. Why on earth did he not shorten his name to Doug?

"I was here alone," Nora said. "Dougwell was at the shops."

How I hated her. I hated the words she used. That masturbatory thing! What an ignorant, stupid thing for her to say. At the shops! What, was she an Englishwoman now?

"Where are Pete's ashes?" I asked. "In a closet? In the garbage?"

Nora hesitated. "Please don't be nasty, Cherry."

"Well?"

"We haven't received them from the crematorium yet," she said.

"I have to go," I said.

Just as I hung up the phone, the doorbell rang. It was a young man, there to read the gas meter in the basement. I let him in and he did his thing. I considered telling him that my brother had hanged himself, but I didn't want to become part of a story he told at the end of his day. Also, maybe it wasn't true. Maybe the phone call hadn't happened or Nora got it wrong. Perhaps it was important that I keep it to myself until I felt more certain about it. I looked at the black phone on the hall desk, for some sort of evidence that it had rung.

The young man left and the phone rang again as I was staring at it. It was Dougwell.

"Cherry? Are you all right?" he asked.

"No."

"I'm so sorry about this. And I'm sorry I didn't take the bull by the horns and phone you sooner."

"It's okay, Dougwell."

"Who are you talking to?" I heard Nora's voice in the background.

Dougwell didn't answer. I guess he was misbehaving by calling me.

"Who is it?" she hissed, closer now. I hung up.

A sick feeling pressed outwards from behind my eyes. It came with the knowledge that I had failed my own brother. I hadn't been able to love him enough. I had feared him. And that fear along with my laziness and not being able to figure out how to know him… I never even imagined there wouldn't always be time.

The doorbell rang again on that November afternoon. This time it was Henry. It was almost five o'clock. We had planned on having a bite to eat and then going to see *The Exorcist*.

I stepped outside and shivered in the cold. There was a misty rain falling.

Henry kissed me. He buried his face in my hair and inhaled. We went inside to bed and I cried while we were doing it. Henry didn't question it; I often cried during sex. I don't know why; it's rare for me to cry at any other time.

"Pete's dead," I said as soon as our breathing returned to normal.

"What?"

"Pete's dead. Nora phoned. He hanged himself," I said. "It might have been an accident."

Henry sat up and stared at me. "You're not kidding me? This isn't some kind of twisted Ring joke?" He didn't believe in the normality of our family any more than I did.

"No."

"When did it happen?"

"On Sunday. Nora phoned me this afternoon." I started to cry again.

"I can't believe we had sex," Henry said, "when you knew that Pete was dead."

"Why?"

"Because. That's why. And I knew Pete too. Christ! Even if I didn't!"

Henry's cruelty stunned me.

"I even had conversations with him," he said. He was comparing his relationship with Pete to the non-relationship I'd had with my brother as though his was superior, which maybe it was.

"Sorry," I said. "I wasn't thinking about the right thing to do. I just wasn't in the mood to talk, you know? Maybe I was just craving comfort."

I didn't know if this was true or not, but I did know I didn't want Henry yelling at me.

"You shouldn't have had to think," said Henry, looking at me as if I was all wrong, somehow. "You should have just told me. Christ."

"I'm sorry," I said again. But I no longer meant it.

"You sucked my dick," Henry said.

"Yes."

"Was that a comfort to you?"

"I don't know."

"What was in your head as you were doing it?"

"Nothing," I said. No, that wasn't right. "I don't know. Pete, I guess."

"Oh, God, Cherry. This is making me sick."

Henry stood up and began to pull his jeans on. His penis was the smallest I'd ever seen it.

I didn't see him again for twenty-two years after that night, except for a few times from a distance at the university and from behind the living room curtains as he pounded on my front door. He tried to make it up with me; even later that same evening he tried. But I wouldn't have it. I couldn't forget the look on his face when I told him Pete was dead. He looked at me as though I were a different species, one that didn't know human rules.

But man, I wasn't thinking straight or I wouldn't have behaved the way I did. I was so hurt and freaked out in my own way. I felt that Henry treated me very shabbily, after all those years of loving me. And I needed to be away from him. It was myself I really wanted a break from—but that wasn't possible, so I took a break from Henry, the next best thing.

I wished I could ask him about the masturbatory phenomenon that Nora had mentioned, but I'd have to find that out from someone else.

Spike was standing expectantly by his dish now so I got up to feed him and think about making something for myself. He squealed and made clicking sounds on the spot with his feet.

A good memory came to me as I mixed up Spike's concoction of wet and dry food.

Nora had told me to find Pete for supper. I must have been thirteen or so, Pete, ten. I went to the river and there he was, crouched down by the edge, watching a beaver repair its home. He was humming something, the theme from *The Rifleman*, I think, (*daa daa da da daaa, daa da da daaa*) and the breeze lifted his fine blond hair. I sat with him for a while before mentioning that it was suppertime. The beaver gnawed and nosed and whapped his tail. Pete laughed once; I think it was at the size of a log the industrious animal was trying to haul. I laughed too, quietly, not wanting to wreck anything about the moment.

I remembered too, that I found a quarter on the walk back from the river. For a second, like I always do when I find money, I believed that this was it; I'd hit the jackpot. I searched the ground for more and there wasn't any, of course. So the disappointment started to set in. It was only a quarter. It would barely buy me a movie. Not even a Walt Disney at the Met; they cost thirty-five cents. Oh well, *Sodom and Gomorrah* was playing at the Lyceum. My spirits picked up again.

The last page of my mother's journal was just gibberish and I gave it no more than a glance. It didn't seem odd to me that her journal ended when and how it did, considering what happened in November of '73.

CHAPTER 20

On a windy warm November evening, not long after Nora's phone call, I walked over to see Eileen, Pete's old girlfriend, at her home on Lloyd Avenue. I wanted to let her know about my brother's death soon after I found out, so I wouldn't have to spring it on her at the Safeway or the drugstore where we sometimes ran into each other. She never failed to ask me about Pete.

I could almost pretend it was a spring night, with the wind and the warmth; I wore a fall jacket and left my parka at home.

Eileen lived in a tiny house with her elderly dad. The doorbell was broken. She gaped at me with her mouth hanging open when she answered my knock. I had never called on her before. She was wearing a nurse uniform made out of what looked to be nylon; it suited her.

The front door opened up directly into the living room. There was no hall there to ease visitors into the house. A gust of sweet November air burst into the room and Eileen yanked me inside.

"Close the door, Cherry. Quickly." She pulled me further into the room by the sleeve of my jacket. "Daddy, this is Cherry Ring, Peter's big sister."

The old man didn't bother with me and I was okay with that. He sat in a wheelchair in front of the television, watching a rerun of *The Brady Bunch*. Part of a meal, maybe breakfast by the look of it, had spilled down the front of his maroon robe and dried there. He favoured one haunch and I wondered if he'd had a hip replacement, like me. For just a second, I envied Pete and the peace of death.

It was a house of closed windows. The smell of urine and elder-sweat mixed with Pine-Sol thickened the stifling air. I wanted to make short work of this chore.

I took off my boots, hoping that Eileen would stop me, but she didn't. When we walked between the wheelchair and the TV, the dad grunted, but that was all I heard from him other than a couple of horking sounds. There were sticky patches on the linoleum and I wished I had worn different socks, darker ones that wouldn't be stained from their experience in this house.

"Excuse the mess," Eileen said. "It's hard to keep up with everything sometimes." She gestured back toward the living room.

She looked exhausted. Looking after the old guy was taking it out of her. He oozed a dank filth that was like another complete presence. Once we were away from him, in the kitchen, things seemed cleaner and tidier, if on the dingy side.

Eileen offered me tea and I declined. Just the thought of it sent waves of nausea through me. I had started to sweat, so I shrugged my jacket off onto a chair.

"Are you on your way to work?" I asked.

"No. I just finished my shift." She smoothed the white skirt of her uniform over her plump thighs.

"Pete's dead," I said. There was no better way to put it. I don't believe in leading up to these things and thereby building the anxiety.

Eileen sank into a kitchen chair and began to weep. Her teeth hadn't grown any since the last time I had seen them.

"I knew it," she wailed. "I knew he would die out there."

The cloth of her nurse outfit felt damp to the touch when I put my hand on her shoulder. She wanted details and there was so much I couldn't tell her. I softened Nora's description and assured Eileen that Pete hadn't wanted to die; it had been an accident. I had struggled with Nora's version of events, but finally chose to believe it because it was easiest that way.

I made my brother's unlikely friend some tea: hot, strong and sweet. When I looked for the milk I recognized Pete's scrawl on a frayed piece of notepaper attached to the fridge. He had written two haiku and given them to Eileen:

the warbler
hits the window
soon to die

Real cheerful.
The other one read:

Birdsong.
Cat in shadow land
Prepares to pounce

When had Pete developed such an interest in the perils of being a bird?

I couldn't imagine anyone except Eileen wanting to fasten such horrible poems to her fridge.

She slurped down the tea and pulled herself together. I found a paper towel and gave it to her.

"If I'm able to find out anything more, I'll let you know," I said, as I picked up my jacket. I was too hot to put it on.

"Thanks, Cherry. I'd appreciate it," she said, "and thanks for making me some tea."

"Will you be all right?" I asked.

"Of course." She blew her nose into the paper towel.

"I'll let myself out."

I scurried past the old man without looking at him again, put on my boots without tying them up, let in another gust of fresh air and stepped out onto the porch. The yard was only about ten feet deep, so I was through the gate and on the front sidewalk in seconds. I didn't stoop to tie my laces or slip into my jacket till I reached the end of the block.

That was the only conversation Eileen and I had about Pete's death. She didn't pester me any further about details. I attributed that to her sensibleness. She trusted that I would give her the information if there was anything to give.

CHAPTER 21

I gave up on Nora completely after Pete's death. At first I skimmed her few namby-pamby efforts at letter writing but when I saw that they were from that same phony simpleton that wrote to me before he died I just looked for Dougwell's message at the bottom and then threw them away. I didn't answer any of them.

One evening in December, in the early days after Pete's second death (I never stopped thinking of the first one as that time in Mr. Whittall's yard), I had a long soak in the tub with jasmine-scented bubbles. Then I sat on my bed and smoothed lotion onto my feet, into the tiny scar on my right instep and the rougher skin of my heels.

Then back to the scar. It was itchy, the kind of itch you get when a cut is healing. I scratched. My memory touched on something from so long ago that I wasn't sure if it was real; I couldn't catch it. My stomach flipped over and I thought for a moment I would vomit. The sensation was quick to leave and a familiar hollowness filled me up. I felt like certain tender parts of me were missing. I couldn't even remember them, so finding them did not seem possible. What took their place was cool and flinty.

I fastened the top on the bottle of lotion and pulled on a pair of cozy socks.

In late April of 1974 I made an appointment with Dr. Bondurant. He was still practising psychiatry in the Manitoba Clinic. And he was still young, probably in his mid-forties by then. I realized with a shock that he must have been in his twenties when I first went to see him about my problems with Pete.

Dr. Bondurant remembered me. He even had my file. He asked about Pete.

I told him about my brother's death and how I blamed myself for so much of what had gone wrong in our family. It was so good to talk to him again.

He offered to take me on as a patient. He still specialized in troubled children, but would make an exception for me because of our history. If I wanted to, I could see him once a week for an hour. I came away from that session feeling positive for the first time in a long while. But I didn't take Dr. Bondurant up on his offer of help. I know I should have; I had so much noise in my head that I needed to get rid of.

We didn't lose touch though. Dr. B. phoned me from time to time to see how I was getting along. He was worried about me; I know he was. He knew that I was wallowing in guilt and shame and anger and he wanted to help me find my way out of it. I called him sometimes too, just to chat. I don't know if he charged the province for our talks or not.

Henry went away again before I forgave him. For the longest time I didn't even know where he had gone.

I hung about with a lot of different guys: students, professors, musicians, nine to fivers, layabouts. Falling in love was never a problem for me. It happened all the time, sometimes with men who loved me back, but not enough, and sometimes with guys who didn't love me at all. Or I loved them a little but not crazy love like I knew it had to be. The opposite happened too. Guys loved me so much they couldn't sleep at night, but they were never the right ones.

Now that I'm older, I know that much of that love wasn't real. But whatever it wasn't, it was what kept me from tumbling into a black pit of loneliness. And it felt real at the time.

As the others came and went, Henry turned into a memory. I heard that he married, that his wife's name was Dolores somebody, that he went east, then west, had a kid or two.

Near the beginning of this story I mentioned that three things happened in the summer of 1995 that caused me to do a lot of reflecting on the past. The first thing was the arrival of Nora's journal in the mail.

The second thing was that on the last Monday in July, Henry Ferris slipped back into my life. I saw him downtown at Mary Scorer Books on Graham Avenue.

He was in the history section, looking at a book about the Korean War. It could have been 1972. He looked the same, except for his hair. It was shorter, of course, and completely white, like Joanne's. The colour increased his handsomeness. His glasses were different too, I realized. In the old days he had worn the round John Lennon type. The new ones had rims and enhanced his face far more. He looked unbelievably beautiful to me. If I could just stay in that moment, I thought—live out the rest of my life gazing upon Henry, not take it any further.

His obvious excitement didn't disappoint me; his face lit up. I had been scared he wouldn't know who I was. That would have killed me.

We went to the Paddle Wheel on the sixth floor of The Bay. I had coffee and Henry had a chocolate milkshake. We sat in the area that had been called the Crinoline Court in the old days. I think only ladies sat in that section when I was a kid. I could be wrong about that, but it seems right.

Henry had moved back to Winnipeg from Edmonton with his two almost-grown kids. They had come back a year before, after his wife Dolores died of lung cancer. She hadn't even smoked. Neither had Henry, so he couldn't blame himself.

"I'm sorry," I said.

"Thanks."

He smiled and I saw the deeply etched lines in his face. They had been invisible to me in the bookstore.

"I've thought of you so often," he said. "You have an unlisted number?"

"Yes. It's because of my column at the paper," I said. "I got a few crank calls."

"I'm not surprised. I've read that column of yours."

"Oh no, not you too. Myrna thinks I'm out-and-out evil. And Joanne thinks I'm asking to be killed."

"You still see Joanne and Myrna?" Henry asked.

"Yeah, quite a lot."

"That's great," said Henry. "I don't really see anyone from the old days."

We discussed the rain barrel baby, as it had come to be known in Norwood—a horrible situation involving the dumping of a little baby. It had taken place earlier in the summer and involved people both of us used to know.

Neither of us had a romantic relationship going on at the present time. We smiled shyly at each other as we got this information out of the way.

Henry had a full professorship at the University of Winnipeg. I told him that my column was my only job and he didn't suggest that I was wasting my education.

He asked about Nora and I told him that she had died a long time ago. He asked about Dougwell and I told him that we were mostly out of touch but that I had been thinking about phoning him lately because of the journal that had come in the mail. I talked about the journal and how I'd been fussing over it. Henry was interested and asked if he would be allowed to see it.

That surprised me, and it took me such a long time to answer that Henry changed the subject back to Dougwell.

"I always liked him," he said. "We named our boy Dougwell."

"You're kidding," I said.

"No. I thought it was a good name and Dolores did too. Even Dougwell himself seems to like it."

"Wow!"

"Most people call him Doug, but he calls himself Dougwell."

This seemed like momentous information to me. I couldn't wait to phone Dougwell and tell him. It was a good reason to call him, a joyful reason.

"That's wonderful, Henry," I said. "What's your other kid's name?"

"Gina. After Dolores' mother."

"That's a good name too," I said.

"Would you like to do something coming up soon?" Henry asked. "Go to a movie or something?"

"I'd love to," I said.

We exchanged phone numbers before we parted. Henry was only mildly surprised that I still lived in the old house on Monck. He went back to the university, where he was teaching a summer course. I went to The Forks, where I sat by the river and drank another cup of coffee.

The next day Henry called.

"May I come over?" he asked.

"No."

In the cool of the morning I had taken every single item out of my kitchen cupboards. It had started out seeming like a good idea to do some cleaning. Now the day was growing hot and the air conditioning had conked out. Plus, Spike had one of those plastic cone-shaped devices around his neck that the vet had attached after surgery on a lump behind his ear. He kept walking backwards and bumping into things.

I explained all this to Henry.

"That's okay," he said. "I'll help you with the cupboards. We'll get it done in no time. And I'd love to meet Spike."

It still didn't sit right with me.

"I don't think so, Henry."

"What is it, Cherry?"

"My house seems very complicated at the moment. And there are remnants here of our last time together."

I could hear him thinking.

"Let's go to a hotel," he said.

"What, you mean for dinner?" I asked.

"Well, we could have dinner. I was thinking about getting a room, say at the Fort Garry, and we could talk and maybe have sex."

"I don't know, Henry. It sounds a bit sleazy to me."

He laughed. "It won't be sleazy if it's us."

"I don't think I'll be able to have sex," I said.

"Well, we can kiss," he said. "I want to kiss you."

Henry stopped kissing me and began to undress, so I did too. I hadn't pictured anything this way. In my imaginings, the man always undoes my buttons for me, kissing my neck and breasts as the material falls away.

The room was dim, but not dim enough. I was suddenly alarmed at the thought of Henry seeing my body again after all these years. There was no way he was going to find my breasts tremendous at this stage, with the new way they had of disappearing when I lay down. He undressed with his back to me, so I hurried with my sundress, flinging it onto a chair and sliding between the cool sheets before he had a chance to see me.

Henry smiled and crawled in next to me. He was hard already, which made me feel good, but scared.

"Your feet are cold," he said when he touched them with his own.

"Sorry," I said.

"You have underpants on," he said.

"Yes."

"You're nervous. I don't want to make you nervous."

"It's okay," I said. "I'm always nervous." I sat up, pulling the sheet with me and fixing a pillow behind my head.

"You didn't used to be."

"Didn't I?"

"Cherry?"

"Yes?"

"I'm thinking this isn't a good idea."

"Did you see my breasts?"

"No." Henry laughed. "Don't be silly. You're beautiful."

He moved to lift the covers from my body, but I stopped him.

"It all seems kind of sudden."

"I'm so sorry, Cherry," Henry said. "I got carried away, seeing you again. But it's not like we're continuing where we left off, is it? Too much time has gone by for that."

Plus, we left off in a pretty nightmarish way, I thought.

"I'd feel better if it were darker and if I were a little bit drunk," I said.

"Well, we can have a drink, can't we?" Henry leapt up and found the key for the mini-bar.

He was so at ease with his nakedness. I envied him that. I had never been that way, even when I was young. He was tanned all over and smooth. Apparently he had a swimming pool in his backyard. He was a little pudgy in places, thank God; I couldn't have stood it if he was perfect.

"What's your pleasure, ma'am?" he asked when he got the little fridge unlocked, something he never would have said twenty-two years ago.

But these new words suited him. I wondered if it was something he said a lot and when the first time he had ever said it was. Would it take me twenty-two years to catch up with the new Henry? Would I get the chance? Did I want the chance?

"Gin and tonic, please," I said to Henry's bum. Imagine his being so comfortable as to bend over that way!

We drank a little and ordered dinner from room service and talked a lot and eventually it did become slightly darker in the room. We still didn't do it, though. It was too soon—thirty years after we had first met. Maybe the taste of the last time was as fresh in Henry's mind as it was in mine. We didn't talk about that.

We did talk about Diesel, the little beagle I had before Spike. Henry had been very fond of Diesel. And he said he was sorry, more than once; he just didn't say what for.

When we walked out of the Fort Garry Hotel onto the warm downtown pavement, the night was just as thick as the day had been. It was a shock after the cool hotel.

"We didn't talk about Pete," he said.

"No."

"Next time?"

"I don't know. Maybe."

Henry hailed a cab for me and I eased into the back seat and rolled down the window.

"He's hard to talk about. Not that I ever try."

Henry crouched and put his hand on top of mine. "I'm sorry," he said again.

"Nothing was your fault."

"One thing was. I shouldn't have left you that way."

"Oh, Henry. We can't talk about this now."

"No."

"Where to, ma'am?" asked the driver.

"Sorry," I said. "Norwood. Monck Avenue. 'Bye, Henry."

"See you soon?"

"For sure."

Henry hailed his own cab. He hadn't brought his car because he figured he'd be drinking. The old cautious Henry.

On the drive home I tried to think about nothing. The driver didn't speak. I'm not very good at thinking about nothing. Every human encounter I have leads to self-doubt, which is just a step or two away from self-hatred. Nothing happened during my hours with Henry that wasn't good, but I didn't feel good; I never feel good. I laugh sometimes. I think things are funny. But I don't feel good.

"Don't pull into the driveway, please," I said. "I'll get out on the street."

I still have a thing about driveways.

CHAPTER 22

The next morning I decided to phone Dougwell. I sat at the dining room table with a cup of coffee and Nora's journal in front of me. Spike was in the backyard on a long leash. I had taken his cone off to give him a break. From where I sat I could keep an eye on him.

A memory came back to me: the phone rang on the night that Nora died nine years ago. I ran downstairs to the desk in the front hall to answer it. I was sure I knew who it was and what he was going to say.

"May I please speak to Sister Mary of the Five Wounds?" a voice said.

That wasn't it.

"What?" I asked.

The caller repeated the question. I couldn't tell if it was a man, woman, child or grownup; it was that strange a voice. The person must have used a distorter of some kind. It was a crank call. Like Myrna used to make.

When I hung up I dialled Nora and Dougwell's number. There was no answer. For no reason I could figure, I knew my mother was dying. She'd be at the hospital and, of course, Dougwell would be with her.

First thing the next morning the phone rang again. That time it was Dougwell and he told me what I already knew. Nora had died the night before.

Sitting at the dining room table now with the little book in front of me, I dialled his number on the coast.

"Have you read the journal?" I asked after the opening pleasantries.

"Pardon?"

"Nora's journal, you jackass." I didn't say the jackass part out loud but I sure wanted to.

"I'm not sure what you're talking about, Cherry. Has something come up?"

By this time I started getting a creepy kind of feeling in my guts. Dougwell wasn't messing with me; he wasn't that kind of man.

"Dougwell, did you not send me Nora's old green journal in the mail?"

"Nora's journal. My. Oh my. I had forgotten all about that little book. I haven't seen it for years. No, I didn't send it to you and to answer your other question, I never did get a look inside of it. I wanted to, mind you, but I never got a chance."

"Where did it come from?" I said aloud to the both of us.

"You know, Cherry, I'm certain that book wasn't with Nora's things when she passed on. I would remember that; it always intrigued me. I don't know if I would have read it or not, but I would have told you about its existence."

I knew this was true.

"There was no return address on the package when I got it," I said.

"How can this be?"

"It can't," I said. "It's impossible."

We listened to each other breathe for a while.

"I'm moving," Dougwell said.

"Moving?"

"Yes, to Penticton. Vancouver's become too difficult for me to get around in."

"That sounds like a good idea, Dougwell. Penticton's a beautiful place." Like I know anything about anywhere.

"My sister lives there."

"I didn't know that."

"No. There's no reason you would."

It was shameful how little I knew of my stepfather.

I remembered Hermione's story of how he had encouraged her when she was in high school.

"Hermione says hello," I said. And she would have if she'd known I was going to phone him.

"Oh, thank you. Hello back. I'm glad you two are friends."

"Yes, me too," I said.

We breathed again for a while.

"She shaved her head."

Dougwell chuckled. "Yes. That sounds like something she would do."

"Are you going to read the journal?" he asked, after another quiet moment or two.

"Yes."

"This is upsetting, isn't it? You don't have to read it if you don't want to, you know. You could discard it."

"I can't not read it. I've already read quite a few parts."

"Where could it have come from, Cherry?"

"I don't know."

Spike began hurling himself against the back door.

"Did she ever talk to you about her childhood?" I asked.

"No. She never talked about her past. She made it quite clear that it was off limits."

Spike rang the doorbell. He managed it from time to time.

I wanted to mention Pete, to speak his name, but I couldn't think of anything to say about him and I couldn't just blurt out his name with nothing else.

There was nowhere to take the conversation. There were no ideas to be had.

"Keep me posted, Dougwell. Send me your new address and phone number."

"I will."

"Really. I'm not just saying that."

I imagined taking a trip to the Okanagan in the fall, accompanying Dougwell and his sister on walks around the lake, eating cherries till my skin turned red, and peaches so juicy I practically drank them.

"Okay, Cherry. I will."

"And phone me if you have any revelations about the journal."

"Ditto."

We murmured our goodbyes and I opened the door for my smart little wiener dog. I should enroll him in agility classes. He could learn to leap through hoops of fire and I could take him on the road and give up my hateful column.

The phone call to Dougwell did me in—confused the hell out of me. And it filled me with feelings of loss and a nudge of hope at the same time. A futile hope, though, one that depended on me and the things I wouldn't do, like visit the Yukon Territory or take Spike to agility school. And the loss was full of things that had never happened, like going out for lunch with my mother.

My coffee was cold. I threw it down the sink.

I forgot to tell Dougwell about Henry's boy having his name. That was going to be the good part of the conversation and I had forgotten it. At least I had mentioned Hermione.

It was August now. Part of my confusion would go away before the month was out, when the arrival of the journal was explained. But I would have preferred being confused to a great deal of what happened in the last week of that month.

CHAPTER 23

That same morning, which was a Wednesday, I phoned an air conditioner repairman and he told me that it would be at least a week before he could squeeze me in. I sensed some pleasure in his voice. So I phoned another one, and then another. Finally I reached someone who could come the next day.

I decided that my next column would be an interview with the owner of an air conditioning repair outfit. I would grill him about the power he enjoyed during heat waves when he turned people away, his sense of enjoyment in the misery and frustration of others.

After scrubbing out all of my kitchen cupboards, I took a shower. As I was towelling off, Henry called and we talked for a while, just about regular day-to-day stuff, like the weather and what we were reading. To our amazement we were both reading riotously funny travel books by Bill Bryson. Before we hung up we made a date for that evening, to go and see *Mighty Aphrodite*.

I put on a cool dress and went down to see how my cupboards were getting along. They were still damp so I looked in the fridge for a while. When I was a kid, Murray used to get after me for that:

standing in front of the fridge for long periods of time, letting the cold air out, causing the mechanism to work too hard.

There was nothing of interest. There was Häagen-Dazs chocolate ice cream in the freezer but it was too early in the day to get started on that. For me it's more of a nighttime thing, like brandy and cigars.

Finally I sat down in the living room and forced myself to have another look at Nora's journal.

Spike walked backwards across the room trying escape his cone.

February 1959
She would sell them both if the price was right.

That was what she wrote.

Nora hadn't loved Pete any better than she'd loved me. She'd had her romantic notion for a while of his being the next Leonard Cohen—a poet's mother would be a good thing to be—but when that vision died I think she must have started to fade away.

It was possibilities that kept her going and when those turned into dreams of what might have been it was time for her to die. It couldn't have been anything but bone cancer. I pictured her real self, the part of her that lived in her marrow, screaming to get out. She squashed it down and painted a picture of a woman who didn't exist, the mother of a pretty family whose members had healthy jobs and creative streaks. The stuff of her bones nearly suffocated and then it reared up in an abnormal show of strength and ate her up.

I was shocked to read in the journal that there had been an older sister who died, a girl before me. She was born dead. Nora moaned about her. Of course she loved her; she was easy to love. But she never gave her a name. She'd just been Baby Girl Ring. I wondered if she had been buried or just thrown away. What happens to stillborn babies? Myrna would know.

There was an entry that told of her indifference toward her remaining children, even Pete. She ignored us both.

1963
> *She doesn't answer their questions or say goodnight at bedtime. It gets easier for her.*

It wasn't just my asking a question that she didn't answer, or telling her a joke that she didn't laugh at. I'm sure all kids' mothers are guilty of those kinds of things. I remembered times when I was a kid when it went much further than that.

Once I was walking home from school at lunchtime—it must have been grade one because I was carrying our class photo and Mrs. Twerdochlib was the teacher in the picture. I could hardly wait to show it to my parents. Murray was at work, of course, but I saw Nora in the yard working in a flowerbed and I broke into a run. When I slowed down as I entered the yard she looked over my head and called out to Mr. Staples across the way, "Hello, Wes! Beautiful day, isn't it?"

He waved and smiled at her, resting his hands on top of his rake.

"We got our school pictures," I said, puffing with exertion and excitement.

Nora stood up, tossed her gardening gloves on the ground and sauntered across the street to talk to Wes Staples, brushing dried leaves from her capri pants as she walked.

Maybe that's where Pete had gotten it, his clean way of dismissing any idea of me.

Inside the memory, I pictured Nora swaying her hips a little to entice Mr. Staples. But I might have invented that part.

I wondered if Nora had hurt Pete as easily as she had me when we were kids. After those first years of his fragile health, I'm not sure there was much between them at all.

Murray made up for Nora the day of the photograph; when he got home he asked me questions about several of the kids in the picture. He fastened it up in the kitchen, making room for it on our bulletin board, and he insisted that I was the prettiest girl in the class. On the day of the photo I had worn a white blouse and my school tunic with the Nordale crest on the front.

I flipped to 1939. October.

> *Luce is skin and bones. Her head is huge. She is going to die and I will be left alone with Mr. Dickson Trent. How could she do this to me?*
> *I try to make her eat. She has stopped taking even water. I see in her black eyes that she knows why I want her alive.*
> *She is giving me to them. I hate her and her wrong death.*

There was a drawing of a monster. It was done in the winter of 1940. Nora would have been eleven years old. It looked like the creature that burst out of someone's stomach in *Alien*. My mum was ahead of her time in her visualization of monsters. For eyes she had cut out a pair from an old photograph and taped them on. The tape was yellow and stiff and came undone when I touched it. I got some fresh Scotch Tape from a kitchen drawer and sat down at the dining room table to fix the eyes neatly back in place: a small effort for my mother. The monster was hideous. Something tweaked inside of me.

The photo album that Roy, the roofer, had found in the attic last winter was in a drawer in the dining room. I turned to the picture of Great-Aunt Luce, the one of her in later years when she no longer looked like me.

Her missing eyes lived in the face of Nora's monster. My mother had cut them out and taped them in place. Her journal monster was Luce Woodman.

No wonder she'd had an aversion to me. My resemblance to her great-aunt made her think she'd given birth to another Luce.

I ached for the aunt. She took what she thought was her only way out and it earned her monster status. It was wrong of her to leave the girl, but... Yes. It was wrong of her to leave the girl, but...it was.

The eyes. I tried to study the eyes. They were too small to be anything but black and without life. I couldn't find evil in something so small.

My eyes are somewhat sad, I guess, with their downward turn, but they are bright and clear. A mixture of good and bad, I hoped, tilting toward good. Not wicked. I would check with Joanne.

> *1939, November*
> *Luce is dead. Darcy Root was with her when it happened.*

The monster should have been Darcy Root, not Luce, I thought.

> *1940, spring*
> *She lay down for the men tonight. She closed her eyes and it wasn't much worse than cleaning out the barn. The same kinds of stinks.*

Nora was talking about herself here. It was the first time she talked about herself as if she were someone else.

> *1951, winter*
> *She bit the girl. While the mother worked to change her, the girl kicked her, knocking the putrid diaper onto the floor. She kicked her while the mother did the creature the favour of trying to make her clean again. Through a mist of red the mother saw her future, as clear as the first morning in a new world. And she didn't want it. She wanted something else: not to be a mother. She bit the tiny quiet girl on the instep of her right foot. The bite drew blood, but nothing she couldn't staunch herself, nothing she couldn't explain away.*

I didn't find it odd or surprising that Nora hadn't wanted to be a mother. I didn't want to be one myself. But I wished with all my heart that it had been someone else's mother and not mine who hadn't wanted children, or who hadn't shifted inside when she held her bouncing baby in her arms for the first time.

Enough with her journal. After reading about the bite I set it aside. It served no purpose except to make me the saddest woman on Monck Avenue.

CHAPTER 24

The third thing to happen that caused me to do so much looking back, and far and away the most momentous of the three, happened on a Thursday night in late August.

Henry and I ate calamari and bread at The Forks. Then we sauntered around and he bought me an amber necklace from a sidewalk vendor. He fastened it around my neck. We walked back to my house where Henry had left his car. He didn't come in. His kids were having a pool party and he figured he should get home to make sure no one drowned or got naked. We kissed through the driver's window and he drove away.

I walked up the front sidewalk to my house. A dark form emerged from the branches of the weeping birch. My blood cooled and a buzzing began in my temples. It formed a living cap on my head.

"Hi, Cherry," he said. It was the first time I'd heard him speak my name.

Pete loomed from the shadows of the birch tree, stepped back again. His white face glowed like a thin moon from the cloak of low branches.

I saw him see me like I did in the hospital after the accident, when he looked at me for the first time since he was one year old. He looked too closely now, as he did then, and I didn't welcome his eyes. I turned away from them and ran inside the house, locking the door behind me. Out of my bedroom window I watched him appear in the radiance of a streetlight. He headed down the avenue toward the river.

For several minutes I stood paralyzed and then I took the phone inside my bedroom closet and called Henry at home. His daughter, Gina, answered. I heard party sounds in the background. Young hoots and laughter.

"He's not home at the moment, Cherry. May I take a message?" she said. "Oh wait! I think I hear him in the garage."

I worried that the phone would get lost in the party. After some long moments Henry said hello and I babbled.

He lives in St. Vital on Victoria Crescent. It's not very far away. I hunkered down among my dresses and shirts. My teeth were chattering and I clenched my jaws till they ached. The doorbell rang.

I raced to meet him and we stood outside on the steps. I apologized for forcing him to come out again.

"It's okay," Henry said. "Everything's fine at home. No one's naked or even drunk. Kids today, I don't know."

He continued talking. My eyes fastened on his mouth but his words lost me. They were familiar but their order seemed wrong. I wanted to forget about why I asked him to come by.

"Are you listening, Cherry? This is important. Do you know who the guy was?" He took both my hands in his. "Was it someone that you've interviewed?"

His words clicked into place like Scrabble tiles.

"It …it was Pete."

"Pete?"

"Yes."

"Pete who?"

"My brother Pete. Our Pete."

Henry sat down on the steps and pulled me down with him. "Our Pete's dead."

"I know he's dead. But Henry, it was him. I saw him. We looked at each other." I shuddered. "He spoke my name."

"Where is he now?"

"I don't know. He went off toward the river. I wasn't going to follow him."

"No, of course not. Let's phone the police."

"Police?"

"Yes."

"No."

"Why?"

"Because Pete's dead and they'll think I'm a crazy woman. Maybe I am a crazy woman. And if he's not dead, he's my brother. I can't call the cops on my own brother."

Henry looked confused. "I don't know what else to do."

"Maybe it'll never happen again," I said. "Maybe it was a mirage."

"What about Frank?" Henry said.

"Frank?"

"Yeah. Frank Foote. He still lives around here, doesn't he?"

"Yes. But what about him?"

"Let's phone him."

"Jesus, Henry. Why?"

"Because he's a cop. Because he was a friend, too, and a really decent guy, as I recall. He wouldn't have to make it an official police thing, but we could use some help. And he'd believe you, wouldn't think you were crazy."

"How do you know?"

Henry took my hand and kissed my fingers.

"Well, for one thing he knew Pete pretty well when we were kids. I don't think he would think this was all that out of character, Pete turning up after he's dead."

I remembered Frank's face peering out from behind the bushes the first time I thought Pete was dead, hanging from Mr. Whitall's tree, a million years ago.

"Maybe you're right," I said. "Pete did have quite a reputation as a magician."

"There you are then," said Henry, as though the rest of our lives had been settled satisfactorily.

"Frank's probably busy," I said. "It's been quite a summer around here, what with the baby being found in Greta's rain barrel and all."

"That's pretty much died down by now, hasn't it?" said Henry.

"I guess so."

I've always known Frank Foote. He's the same age as me, so we were often in the same classes at Nordale School and then later at Nelson Mac.

Frank had a crush on me in grade two. Once, at the Norwood Community Club, I was standing on my head during a dance class and he rushed in and kissed me on the lips. He was called Frankie in those days.

His crush didn't last. I watched him stop loving me when he heard me call my brother Assface. My meanness scared him away.

So Henry phoned him out of the blue and I listened on the extension in the laundry room. It was late, almost midnight, and Frank was flossing his teeth. He told Henry that. It's the last thing he does before looking in on each of his kids and crawling into bed.

I could tell Frank was glad to hear from Henry, but leery, as he listened to what he had to say.

"I want to help, Henry," Frank said, "but I can't, unless you make a call to the police."

"Why?"

"Well, it sounds like one of those situations where you want a cop, but don't want it to be a an official police situation."

"Yes."

"I get a lot of those, mostly from people in the neighbourhood. And I swore after the last one that I wouldn't do it again."

"Oh," said Henry.

There was a long pause and I listened to someone's breathing, not knowing if it was Henry or Frank. Then I realized it was me and I put my hand over the mouthpiece.

"Why are you so hesitant to call the actual police?" Frank asked.

"Because nothing has actually happened," Henry said. "No crime, as such."

"Well, it sounds like trespassing to me. Or stalking. Mischief?"

"But Cherry is sure it was her brother."

"Pete."

"Yeah. And Pete's dead."

"Yes."

Frank was quiet again, waiting for Henry to continue, I guess, but there was nothing more to say.

"I see what you mean," Frank said. "It's complicated."

"Cherry is worried the police will think she's crazy," Henry said.

"Where is she now?" Frank asked.

I held my breath.

"She's in the laundry room listening to us on the extension."

I could have killed him.

"Thanks very much, Henry," I said.

Frank chuckled. "Hi, Cherry."

"Hi, Frank. I feel like an idiot."

"Don't," Frank said. "How's this for an idea? I'll come to see you, but not till tomorrow morning."

He sounded firm in his decision. I could feel Henry not wanting to push it, wanting to agree, hoping I wouldn't say anything to wreck it.

"Thanks, Frank," I said. "That'd be great."

CHAPTER 25

Henry stayed the night but left first thing in the morning without even a cup of coffee. He trusted his kids but as he said, you never know.

I sat at the dining room table with my coffee and the Friday *Free Press*. But I didn't get much reading done.

There were three main things I wondered about, now that I knew Pete was alive. First, what had really happened with his hanging? Did he try to hang himself and fail? Or did he fake it, like that other time, in Whitall's yard? Or was it an accident that Nora found in time? Or was the whole damn episode invented?

It seemed important for me to know if he had wanted to die, however briefly. And I still didn't know how far the scam went. Was it just me and Dougwell and Winnipeg that were lied to, or were Pete's friends and acquaintances in Vancouver led to believe he was dead as well?

And what about Dougwell? That was the second thing I wondered. I couldn't bear to think he had been in on it, but how could I not consider it?

The third main thing I wondered was why Nora told me that Pete hadn't been quite dead when she found him, how she had watched him die. But how could I ever get an answer to that? It had to have been just for her own entertainment.

Then there were the secondary things I wondered: Where had Pete been all these years? How had he been living? Did he know that Nora was dead? Was she dead?

There was a knock on the front door. I looked out the window and saw a *Green Guys'* truck. That's the company I had hired earlier in the summer to try and do something about the state of my grass. They hadn't been very successful so I didn't hire them for a second treatment.

"Yes?" I said to the unsmiling young man at the door.

"I'm here to do the aeration portion of your lawn package," he said, and showed me the order form with my name and address typed neatly in the appropriate places.

"That's odd," I said. "I didn't order this work."

"Well, would you like it done, now I'm here?" he asked, and I realized that this was an underhanded sales pitch.

"No!"

"Are you sure?"

"Of course I'm sure. And I'm also disgusted that you would try to trick me into having my lawn aerated. Did someone put you up to this? Your boss maybe?"

"Yeah," he said.

"Are you sure?"

"No."

He'd gone red in the face and started backing away.

"So it was your bright idea?"

My voice was loud now and I could see Mr. Widener staring from two doors down. Mitzi started to bark; Spike was leaning hard against my legs and he began a low growl deep in his throat.

"Prick!" I said quietly.

"What?" said the Green Guy.

"Nothing."

"What did you call me?"

"Nothing," I said and was already regretting the whole unfortunate incident. Why couldn't I have handled it like a Zen master? If he'd gone to Joanne's house she would have smiled at him and given him a glass of water.

"You'll live to regret this," he said and marched toward his truck.

"Great," I said.

He turned around. "What?"

"Nothing."

This encounter upset me terribly. I went back inside the house and locked the door behind me. Spike brought two clean rags up from the basement and left them by my chair in the living room. He looked at me expectantly. I am never quite sure why he brings me bits of cloth, but I think of it as a gift; it always feels like one.

"Thank you, Spike," I said, and lifted him up so I could kiss his soft forehead.

He joined me in my chair where I tried to do the type of breathing we would be learning at my yoga class; I'd been to the orientation meeting. I breathed through alternate nostrils but I got mixed up. So I just breathed deeply but normally for a few minutes till my heart slowed down. Then I warmed up my coffee, found the phone and my little phone book and sat back down.

I called Dougwell at his sister's house in Penticton and told him about the events of the previous night. I wanted to talk to him about all the things that were nagging at me, but it wasn't the right time for those kinds of questions. His shock at Pete's being alive was so great that I worried I might have damaged his heart with the news.

"Would you like me to come, Cherry?" he asked after a moment.

"No, Dougwell. Henry's here to help me. And I think we're even going to call the police. I'm a bit scared, but there's no reason for you to be here."

"Henry. That's good. Are you sure about me not coming?"

"Yes. I'd love to see you, but not now. Maybe I'll come and visit later in the fall?" This seemed a little far-fetched but not impossible.

I could hear what must have been Dougwell's sister in the background.

"Sit down, Dougie," she said. "Take a sip of water."

We decided to talk again later in the day. I had so many questions.

But he called me right back. He must have sensed my need to know certain things.

Dougwell stressed that he hadn't been home at the time of Pete's non-death. The ambulance had been and gone according to Nora, the basement had been cleaned up and all that was left was my mother in a heap of tears. He was worried that I would think he was in on it.

My suspicions about him didn't stay with me for long.

Nora had taken care of the arrangements. The non-arrangements. For all either of us knew there hadn't been an attempted suicide, an accident, or a faked hanging. There was just a mother and son chat. It was most probable that Pete had never planned to die. This both comforted me and scared me to death. Why had they done it?

As far as Nora's embellishing the death scene went, Dougwell couldn't answer my questions about that. I shouldn't have even asked.

If I had been there and the charade had played itself out, I would have gotten to the bottom of it. I would have demanded to see my brother's body. Or something. Nora's word would never have been enough. How could it have been enough for Dougwell? He'd been under her spell, I guess. And not connected to Pete like I was. By the time Nora told me about Pete's death he had supposedly been cremated already. I should have asked for proof: a certificate of death. Why hadn't I? Dougwell hadn't been the only one under her spell.

I didn't want to say what came out next but I couldn't stop myself.

"You were with Nora when she died, weren't you, Dougwell?" I asked.

"Yes," he said, "I was. And I don't blame you for asking."
We said our goodbyes again and promised to talk soon.

Nora's journal sat where I had left it on the dining room
table. I hadn't looked at it since I read the part about her biting my
instep.

I flipped to the Vancouver years.

When I turned to the back page I realized that I had looked
at it before, but had taken it for gibberish. I looked more closely
now and suddenly realized what I was looking at.

1973

*Pegetege egis egin jegaegil. Hege wegas bregoegught egup
egon chegargeges egof segelleging dregugs tego meginegors.
Hegeregoegin. Egit wegas thege egotheger wegay
egaregoegund, begut nego egonege begelegiegeveges hegim
begut mege. Thege regottegen kegids wegerege segelleging
egit tego Pegetege. Hege megight bege egawegegy fegor ega
vegeregy legong tegimege.*

*Hegow wegoeguld egi egexplegaegin hegis egabsegencege
fregom megy legifege tego thege wegomegen whego
cegomege fegor bregidgege egand begoegok clegub? Whegat
wegoeguld egi tegell thege negeegighbegoegurs whegen
thegeegy nego legongeger segeege hegim egaregoegund?
Egand hegis egold fregiegends fregom hegomege, whego
tegurn egup egon egoegur degoegorstegep. Hegow cegoeguld
egi egexplegaegin tego thegem hegis whegeregeegabegoeguts
egand wegatch thegem regtegurn egeegast wegith tegaleges
egof egoegur fegamegilegy's shegamegege?*

*Wege hegavege cegomege egup wegith egan egidegeega
begetwegeegen thege twego egof egus. Degeegath!
Negobegodegy wegill egeveger knegow
Megatsqeguegi.*

The reason I hadn't gotten it at first was that when my friends and I had used this code in the sixties we had never written it down. It was a verbal communication. We added the two letters *eg* in front of every vowel, including y's, and made sure none of the vowels were silent. We found it a fairly easy way to talk in secret around adults or other people who we didn't want to include in our conversations, like little brothers or sisters, people like that. It was rude and mean, I guess. I don't remember if we made it up or stole it.

Imagine Nora having figured it out! Or maybe it was something she already knew about, like pig Latin. Maybe it wasn't as ingenious as we thought. I couldn't tell, looking at it now.

Translation:
Pete is in jail. He was brought up on charges of selling drugs to minors. Heroin. It was the other way around but no one believes him but me. The rotten kids were selling it to Pete. He might be away for a very long time.

How would I explain his absence from my life to the women who come for bridge and book club? What would I tell the neighbours when they no longer see him around? And his old friends from home, who turn up on our doorstep. How could I explain to them his whereabouts, and watch them return east with tales of our family's shame?

We have come up with an idea between the two of us. Death! No one will ever know.

Matsqui.

The Matsqui Institution in Abbotsford. I'd heard of it. So Nora had helped Pete lie because he went to jail—because of the shame involved in that. She'd had no fear of tempting the gods with her only son—no fear of dangling him before them in that way. His death sat better with her than a stint in jail. It was kinder to her image. And Pete—he went along for the ride; he just didn't care.

I turned to the monster page and reached for a white pen. Underneath Nora's alien I wrote:

Gregeegat-Egaeguntegiege Legucege

Translation:
Great Aunt Luce

Then I phoned Dougwell back and told him about this latest revelation.

CHAPTER 26

It was noon when Frank Foote knocked on my door. I was sitting at the dining room table staring at a piece of toast. I shuffled into the kitchen and we looked at each other through the screen.

"May I come in, Cherry?" Frank asked.

"Sure. Sorry, Frank. Come on in."

"I apologize for not making it sooner," he said. "Sadie dislocated her elbow and I had to run her over to the hospital to get it popped back in place."

"Oooh. That sounds painful," I said. "Is she okay?"

"Yup. She's fine. It's happened before so she knows it's not the end of the world, even though it hurts a lot."

"Poor little kid," I said.

"Yeah. The doctor complimented her on her toenail polish though, so she's feeling pretty good about things now."

I laughed. "Would you like some coffee, Frank? It's already made."

"No thanks," he said. "I'm all coffeed up."

He held one of his big hands out in front of him, horizontally, so we could both watch it vibrate.

I led him into the dining room where we sat down at my big oak table.

"Toast, then?" I said. "I'm not going to eat this."

I pushed it towards him along with the Malkin's cherry jam. He spread a little jam on the cool toast and took a bite.

"Mmm," he said.

"Yes, I know," I said. "It's from the Tall Grass Bakery."

I watched Frank chew. He looked so innocent, and so comfortable in a nervous kind of way. Probably I made him nervous. I wished that I were June Cleaver. Frank could be Ward. Wally and Beaver could be grown up and successful in their chosen fields.

"So Pete came back from the dead to pay me a visit," I said.

Frank swallowed his first bite. "It must have been a shock for you to see him again."

"To say the least."

"So you thought he was dead." Frank took another bite and chewed slowly.

"Yes. Didn't you?"

I thought everybody knew. It was the type of thing that people love to know.

He nodded. Frank wouldn't speak with his mouth full.

"I had heard," he said, wiping the edge of his lips with a napkin that he took from a little pile on the table. "It was a long time ago now, wasn't it?"

"1973," I said.

The phone rang and I went out into the hall to answer it. It was Myrna, according to the call display, but she hung up after two rings. She must have had a change of heart or a stiff at the door.

"Remember that time Pete pretended to hang himself in Mr. Whitall's front yard?" I sat down again across from Frank.

"Yes, I do remember that," Frank said. "It's as though he doesn't get how serious death is for most people; he plays with it like it's a game."

"I think it's more aggressive than that." I sighed.

"You and he had a fairly tumultuous relationship as I recall," Frank said.

"More of a non-relationship, really. He pretty much pretended that I didn't exist."

"Christ, that's not how I remember it," Frank said. "He used to talk about you all the time, at least when we were very young. By the time we got to high school he and I didn't really hang around together much anymore."

"Pardon?"

Frank looked at me. "The whole thing?"

"No. The part about how he talked about me."

"He did talk about you a lot. He was always planning some sort of trick to play on you."

"Well, fuck."

Frank took another bite, so I gave him a few minutes while I processed this new information about my brother. It had never occurred to me that he would have talked about me to anyone else, if he hadn't talked to me.

But then I remembered seeing Pete and Duane playing ball together the day after I lost my virginity. And Pete's presence at the party the night before.

"He loathed me," I said.

"That's pretty strong," said Frank. "But he did have a bone to pick with you, that's for sure."

He didn't look at me when he said that and I had the wild idea that he knew about my biting Pete. Could he know about that? How could he know about that?"

"I think it had to do with you calling him Assface," Frank said. "He must have really hated that. I know I would have."

"Do you know why I called him that?" I couldn't say the name out loud. My face felt hot.

"It had something to do with a scar on his cheek, didn't it? Skin was grafted from his butt onto his face after he took a bad fall. Something like that?"

"Something like that, yeah. It was mean of me to give him that name, wasn't it? It really caught on."

"Yes. I guess it was mean, but you were just a kid. Kids seem to have to be taught not to be mean."

"You have three kids, right, Frank?" I needed to change the subject.

"Yup, three." He whipped out his wallet and laid it on the table. Three faces smiled up at me through cloudy plastic.

"This is Emma; she's fourteen. Garth, our boy. And Sadie, the youngest." Frank smiled. "She's the boss."

"They're a fine-looking bunch of kids."

I got up and moved to the window seat where I could concentrate on the chickadees in the apple tree. I could hear Frank folding his pictures back into his wallet.

"Do you want to make an official report about Pete?" he asked.

"No. I'm sorry, Frank. Henry shouldn't have phoned you. There's nothing to be done."

"I'm sorry, too," Frank said. "And I don't really know what to suggest. Why don't you let me know if he turns up again?"

He wrote all his phone numbers on a serviette and anchored it with the cherry jam. He kept a pen in his shirt pocket.

"Your mother passed away, right?" Frank stood up to go. "She's no longer around?"

"Yeah, a long time ago."

"So, it's just you and Pete."

"Yeah, a real well-rounded family."

"Well, families come in all shapes and sizes, don't they?"

"We have a stepfather," I said. "Dougwell Jones."

"I remember him," said Frank. "He was a really nice guy."

"He still is," I said. "I never see him though. He lives in Penticton."

"You should make the effort," Frank said. "He might be of some comfort to you when things get tough."

"Thanks for coming, Frank."

It was time for him to go. I didn't want his advice. I didn't even want to be June Cleaver anymore. A moment ago I wanted to tell Frank that Henry had named one of his kids Dougwell, but now I felt too low to speak.

Later on in the afternoon I took Spike for a walk. He cheered me up with his gently flapping ears and his love of sticks. It's easy for me to imagine how good that rough stick must feel against his teeth and gums.

The Green Guy was spraying a yard on Birchdale Avenue. I stopped and watched from a short distance away. I figured when he saw me I'd give him a friendly wave to try to make up for the hard feelings from earlier in the day. I explained what we were doing to Spike, who remained very still. He thought we were trying not to be seen.

The Green Guy finally looked in our direction and I waved and smiled. Spike remained motionless but his eyes took in my movements. The guy didn't wave back.

Fuck him! I turned on my heel. Spike reared up and turned, too, and we walked smartly away.

CHAPTER 27

It was the Saturday of the Castle party, two days after Pete's reappearance. Quint Castle Jr. is the wealthiest man in the Norwood Flats, as his dad, Quint Sr., was before him. The old man made his money in the courier business, starting out on a bicycle delivering documents between offices in downtown Winnipeg. He saved enough to buy a car and then a van; the van became a fleet and now Castle Courier has its own hangar of planes at Winnipeg International Airport.

Quint Castle Sr. is dead now, but his only son, Quint, whom I've known forever, slid nicely into his father's shoes as Norwood's only mogul.

Every summer he and his wife, Virginie, have a party at their home by the river and invite everybody in the neighbourhood. I don't know what they would do if everyone came. Cope, I guess. Usually fifty or so guests turn up. I think there were over a hundred one year; that was the record.

It was a tradition started by Quint Sr. and his wife. I remember times when Joanne and I were kids that we would give one another boosts up the rough wooden fence and peer at the revellers with their tanned bodies and their plinking ice cubes. They lounged around the sparkling pool and always there would be shrieks of hilarity as some jokester leapt in with his clothes on, or tossed in a woman whom the wine had made a little too free.

Nora and Murray, and later Dougwell, went on several occasions. It was right up my mother's alley. She would have loved to live inside one of those tinkling ice cubes at the very centre of the party. She loved the attention of men and they swarmed her like galumphing bumblebees. In my constant prayers to the god of my childhood I asked that he would please never let my mother get into any real trouble. That he would hold at bay the jealous wives as their husbands made fools of themselves at my mother's feet. I could picture some woman, Mrs. Castle, maybe, flying at my mother in a rage, punching her in the throat till the men hauled her off. As far as I know, there was never an incident.

Quint Jr., like Frank, is the same age as me. We were often in the same class at school, and for a couple of summers were pretty good friends. We played Robin Hood and Maid Marian, caught frogs and lit small fires at the river. It was before we were old enough to think about kissing each other.

I always go to the parties. I guess I have that much of Nora in me. The event is never as good as the idea of it, but I always make a point of standing back during the evening, back to the fence or the bushes by the river bank to see it as I saw it then, when all the summer in the world seemed to be right there before my eyes.

Joanne had to talk me into going with her this time. Her husband, Grant, never goes; it's not his thing, he says.

I'd told Henry I wasn't going. I didn't feel up to it, with Pete's resurrection so new. It would keep me from getting into the spirit of the thing.

But Joanne thought it was important for me to get out, to get away from my ghost.

"He's not a ghost," I said.

We were in my bedroom and she was rummaging through my closet for something I could wear.

"So you say." She didn't quite believe me.

I ran downstairs to get Nora's journal and showed her the page where she had written in our secret code.

"Jesus," Joanne said.

"Yeah."

"So he's been alive all this time." She sat down in a pile of clothes. "God, no wonder you're so weirded out."

"Yeah."

"Frank will help you, Cherry," she said. "He was so nice to Greta during the rain barrel thing. She pretty much fell in love with him."

"I'm not so sure. He doesn't seem all that sharp to me," I said. "Plus, I don't think he wants to get involved."

"He will though."

"I don't know. This summer has been really tough for him. The dead baby thing hit him really close to home. One of his kids was hurt."

"Jesus. I didn't know that."

"No. They tried to keep it quiet."

"Hurt how?"

"I don't know."

"Which kid?"

"The oldest one, Emma."

"Is she okay?"

"I think so, but it's been quite a summer for them."

"Well, it's turning out to be quite a summer for you too. And Frank's a cop."

Joanne found a dress and held it up against me.

"This is the one," she said. "Cool, comfy and becoming."

It was a dress I'd worn just twice. It fits me nicely but has no sleeves, so I worried about my arms, but they were brown and that night they looked okay. Maybe I'd lost weight over the past day.

Bare legs and sandals. Silk underwear. What was I saving it for?

"I told Henry I wasn't going," I said.

"You could phone him and tell him you changed your mind."

"I don't want to," I said.

"Well, don't then," Joanne said. "You can blame me for making you go at the last minute."

We had gin and tonics at my house before we left. We felt pretty good about how great we looked and we put Lucinda Williams on the CD player.

Joanne and I walked over to the huge house on Lyndale Drive.

"We can drink as much as we want tonight and not worry about driving home," I said.

"Don't overdo it, now," Joanne said. "We don't want you barfing in the bushes like you did that time."

"That was in the eighties!"

"Yeah? So? You're too old to be barfing from drinking."

"It was in the eighties!"

"You were too old in the eighties, too."

We walked through the gate to the backyard. There were people in the pool already, with bathing suits on. Some people had brought children. This had never happened before and I didn't like it. It was supposed to be an adult affair.

Quint was talking to the bartender, who was slicing limes for people like me. We walked over and I plunked my Bombay Sapphire gin on the bar.

"You didn't have to bring that," Quint said and kissed me on the temple. "Hi, Jo," he said. He didn't kiss Joanne.

"Gin and tonic please," I said to the young man.

"Comin' up."

"Amici's?" I asked.

"Yeah," said Quint.

Amici's is the wonderful restaurant that he and Virginie usually get to cater these affairs.

Joanne slipped away to talk to someone who had just arrived.

"Why are there kids here?" I asked.

"I don't know. Some people just brought them. I couldn't very well tell them to go away. I don't even know them."

"Whose fault is that?" I asked. "Who sends invitations to everyone in the land?"

Quint grinned. "It's okay. As long as they don't stay too long. We want to be able to get loud and obnoxious."

Virginie motioned to Quint from across the yard and he excused himself.

The bartender handed me my drink and I looked around for someone I knew. I didn't like the feel of the party. It was dark in the shrubs by the river; there could have been a little boy in there too close to the water. He could have been taking sips from his mum's Alabama Slammer. It wasn't any good; it felt like the kind of party where someone would die.

Eileen was splayed out in a lawn chair talking to Virginie and Quint. When her dad had finally died she'd sold the tiny house on Lloyd Avenue and bought one on Pinedale. So she's still around.

I didn't want to talk to her. She'd been really good about not asking about Pete since I'd told her about his death, but she had acquired a smugness over the years that made me want to knock her down. What the hell did Eileen have to be smug about? I'd wondered it more than once over time but now as soon as I thought it, I knew the answer.

"No, Klaus, no!" A woman shouted.

And a stout man, in bright yellow swimming trunks, let out a holler and cannonballed into the deep end of the pool. He drenched my dress.

"You great fucking moron!" I shouted.

He didn't hear me; he was under water. But two mothers did. They reached instinctively for their children and looked at me with shock on their faces. One mother covered her child's ears with both hands. He shook her off.

Quint and Joanne both came over to run interference. They made an attractive couple. They had gone together for a time in high school, but they fought all the time. My theory was that Quint was too much like his dad: a head of the family type of guy who wanted the little woman at his side. Joanne didn't fit the mould and fought when he tried to squeeze her into it. And as I mentioned earlier, Quint kissed like a dead man. He had gone off to university in Montreal where he met Virginie and brought her home. Maybe she'd had better luck than Joanne teaching him how to kiss.

"Do you want to go home and change your dress?" Joanne asked me now.

"No. It's okay. It'll dry fast in this heat."

The mothers and Quint were talking, looking my way now and then. The children put their shoes on and they left soon after.

Klaus stood next to the woman who had shouted his name. She was gesturing and he looked puzzled as though to say, what's the big deal? His jiggly stomach lopped over the waistband of his bathing suit and he rubbed it with one hand.

Quint came over to where Joanne and I were standing.

"Do you want to borrow something of Virginie's to put on?" he asked.

"Cherry's three times her size," said Joanne. "You crazy idiot," she added, quietly.

I chuckled. "You could divide me in three and I'd still be bigger than her."

"What?" Quint said. He didn't get it. I guess he thought all women were the same size.

"Nothing. No, I'm fine."

"Cherry, Eileen has been telling us that Pete's back," Quint said and touched my arm.

The touch of his hand felt like a hot iron on my skin and I jerked my arm away. His words ricocheted around inside my brain: Pete's back...Pete's back...Pete's back...The party grew quiet, or seemed to.

I looked over at Eileen and saw that her face was huge. And the smugness was permanent; the smugness was her life. My legs wobbled as the certainty seized me. Not only had Pete contacted Eileen in a real sense, not just scaring her by looming out of the night, but he had been in touch with her all along. She had always known that he was alive, at least, almost always. Her grief had been real enough the night I told her that he had died. But she knew soon after that he wasn't dead. She'd been in contact with him all this time and had kept it from me. The smugness. Of course.

Joanne slipped her arm through mine.

"Yes," I forced myself to speak. "Not only is he back. He's alive."

I couldn't take my eyes off Eileen. I imagined my fist crashing into that mouthful of tiny teeth. With minimal trouble I could ruin her face.

"Let's go," Joanne said.

Quint was left gaping after us. He meant no harm; he didn't know anything.

Once we hit the front yard I sat down on the grass and leaned against a giant rock of weathered granite someone must have hauled in from Lake Winnipeg.

"Joanne?"

"Yes?"

"Would you please go back and get the gin?"

"I can't do that."

"Yes, you can."

"No, I can't."

"I'll give you twenty-five dollars."

"I don't want twenty-five dollars."

"What if Eileen has a drink of our gin?"

There was an ill wind blowing through me. I think Joanne could probably feel it. She walked back around the side of the house and returned in a few moments with the blue bottle.

"How'd it go?" I asked.

"I don't think anyone noticed," she said. From her other hand she produced a pack of Players King Size Extra Light that had barely been cracked. "Look what else I got," she said.

We laughed and leaned against the rock long enough to finish two cigarettes apiece. We drank straight gin from the bottle, but not very much.

"Prick!" I said.

"Who?" asked Joanne.

"I don't know. Pete. Eileen. Everybody, except us. Let's do something fun," I said.

"Like what?"

"Let's climb the fence at the pool in the flood bowl and go for a swim."

"What about bathing suits?" Joanne said.

"We'll go in our underwear," I said, "like Dory Preston and Janny Warren did in 1963."

"Do you remember absolutely everything anyone ever did?"

"Almost."

"I'll do it if we go home and get our bathing suits," said Joanne.

We never got to the pool.

The sirens were so close I felt them under my skin. We ran. I saw the smoke and as we got closer, the flames. Spike. My scalp separated from the slippery bone beneath it; I felt the wind on my skull.

My garage was on fire; my rickety old garage with the wooden door that moved sideways, with the hose winder-upper that Murray built.

I unlocked the front door of the house and looked for Spike. He was under the couch with just his little pointed nose poking out. When he knew it was me he leapt into my arms. He was quivering and crying. I tried to calm him. I had to go outside. He wouldn't let me put him down so I carried him with me.

There was no saving the garage but the firefighters contained the blaze with no problems and there was no other damage.

It was a suspicious fire and it was obvious they were thinking in terms of hooligans. They did mention the number of flammable liquids in my garage, the repeated small explosions. I didn't even know what was in some of those containers. They had been there since Dougwell and even Murray, in some cases, I'm sure.

The police arrived. They wanted to know if I had any idea how the fire might have started. I didn't feel up to telling them about all my enemies: Pete, all the people I had interviewed over the years and their families and friends, Darius Widener, the mothers of the little boys I had sworn in front of that very night, Klaus, the Green Guy.

"No," I said.

Joanne took me aside. "Wouldn't this be a good time to mention Pete?"

"No."

"Why not?"

"I can't tell the police about my own brother. And what would I tell them, anyway? My brother stood beside the birch tree in the front yard?"

"You told Frank."

"Yeah, but he's not like a real cop," I said. "And Henry made me."

"His being dead might be of interest to them," Joanne said. "I should make you tell them about Pete."

We were both covered in debris from the fire. She knocked a few black bits from my shoulders.

"No, you shouldn't," I said. "Do you think my dress is ruined?"

"Probably not; I think it'll be okay."

I watched two firefighters lift Murray's hose contraption, carry it over to the oak tree and set it down.

"Good thing the hose wasn't attached or it would have melted and caused quite a stink," said one.

"Yes. Good," I said.

"There's Mr. Widener," said Joanne. She motioned with her head toward the lane.

He walked over to us. Spike stopped shaking and growled. This was an enemy he understood.

"Hell of a thing," Mr. Widener said.

"Yes, isn't it?" I said, giving him what I hoped was a knowing stare.

I have had more than one run-in with Darius Widener because his dog barks non-stop in a high-pitched voice. It drives me insane at all hours of the day and night. I could hear the dog now.

"Mitzi wasn't able to scare off the firebugs," I said.

"What?"

"Mitzi. Her constant shrill barking." My voice rose and Joanne put a hand on my arm.

"Can you not hear her?" I asked.

Mr. Widener listened carefully for a moment. No listening was necessary; Mitzi's yelp was a constant backdrop to life on our street.

"Hmm, I guess something must have caught her attention," he said.

I'm not against a dog barking. Spike barks sometimes, if he has a good reason. It's not a pleasant sound, but it is nowhere near the eardrum-piercing shriek that comes out of Mitzi Widener for no reason other than that her master is an idiot.

Heaving a sigh, I walked out to the lane. There must have been fifty people gathered in groups at varying distances. All those who weren't at the Castles' party, I guessed. Each to his own. I wondered if the person who started the fire was among the watchers. I scanned the crowd for Pete's face.

CHAPTER 28

Spike and I lazed in bed the next morning. My body was heavy with unease. For some reason it was my swearing at Klaus, the human cannonball, that was at the forefront of my mind. I dragged myself downstairs for coffee, then crawled back into bed with the phone and little phone book.

First I called my insurance company and left a message. Then Quint, to apologize for my language in front of the visiting kids. He couldn't believe I thought it even warranted a phone call. He'd heard about the fire and offered help if I should need it. When I hung up on Quint, someone from the insurance company phoned me back. It being a Sunday, I was amazed and grateful.

My poor old garage was a pile of rubble out back. Some stuff survived the fire, but I didn't feel up to scrabbling through everything. My insurance would cover someone coming to clean up the whole mess, so I didn't have to deal with it. They just had to wait for the say-so from the fire department. Because no one had been hurt in the fire it wouldn't be a priority for the cops.

Next I called Henry and told him about the fire and about what I had decoded in Nora's journal. He wanted to come over, but I was so tired I asked him not to. I planned on doing not much of anything and squeezing in a nap or two.

When Spike and I returned from a walk by the river that evening, we took the front street so I didn't have to look at the garage. I found a note sticking out of my mailbox.

Cherry,
> *Let's talk. I'm staying at the Norwood Hotel. Room 503.*
> *Anytime.*
>> *Your loving brother,*
>> *Pete*

I didn't know what to do. There was nothing I wanted less than to talk to Pete after a lifetime of not talking to him.

Security lights turned on and off as I walked down the lane between Monck and Claremont. A bad feeling was firmly settled in my guts. Mitzi barked even though I was nowhere near. I wondered if other dogs, besides Spike, disliked her.

I cut through Coronation Park; it was quicker than walking around it, and I was less visible. At 11:30 at night the cops could stop me, figure they were doing me a favour by offering to drive me home.

Just going to see my brother at the Norwood Hotel, I would say. Sure, little lady. Hop in and we'll save you from yourself. That's how it would go.

When I slipped between the bowling alley and the once-magnificent house next door to it, I wondered who had lived there, way back when, and how they had felt when the bowling lanes had gone up and spoiled their view.

A small parking lot and then Horace Street. A broken Mateus bottle glinted in the scruffy grass next to someone's garbage can. I wanted to use its neck to slice a throat. I boosted myself over the low fence behind the hotel parking lot. My hip hurt.

The night clerk didn't look up when I made a beeline for the elevator. I knew I wasn't doing anything blameworthy, but I felt furtive and on the wrong side of things. If I were a good and normal person I would be drifting off to sleep at home in my clean bed.

I knocked at room 503 and Pete answered immediately, before my knuckles left the door. It startled me and did nothing to rid me of my bad feeling.

He was not wearing a shirt. I found this distasteful. He was skinny and hairless and I knew he would be clammy to the touch. I couldn't recall having ever been in contact with his bare skin, not since that day in 1954. There were needle welts on the insides of his arms; one spot looked infected. He didn't try to hide any of this from me.

"Cherry," he said. "Come in."

The place reeked of stale smoke and his body stank of old vegetable soup, dirty soup, like what you smell when you walk down the lane behind the Remand Centre on Kennedy Street. It blasts out of the exhaust pipes.

"You're not dead," I said.

Pete smirked. His hair was so greasy I couldn't tell if it was still blond.

"Do you want a drink?" he asked.

"Yes."

I found a glass, one that hadn't been unwrapped yet. He poured a good amount of rye whiskey into it. There was another glass, one with orange lipstick on it, on the bedside table. I was not the only visitor he'd had. I'd never seen Eileen wear lipstick at all, let alone orange, so he must have been in touch with someone else. Or maybe he had hired a hooker. I had little understanding of Pete's needs or desires.

"You're not having one," I said.

He smiled. His once beautiful white teeth had gone brown. A front one was chipped and there was a dark brown line down the middle of another. I could see that some were missing toward the back of his mouth. I wondered if he was conscious of how horrible he looked. Maybe he didn't see what I saw when he looked in the mirror.

"Do you have any Coke or anything?" I asked. I like rye all right, but not by itself.

He didn't respond.

I took a gulp and coughed.

"Why have you come back now?" I asked.

There must be a question he will answer, I thought.

He sat on the bed, facing a wall.

I moved to the window and looked out at the night. Nothing much happens on Marion Street on a Sunday. A cop car cruised by. Pasquale's was closed and so was the pub downstairs. One straggler lurched across the street to his home in the seniors' residence. He stopped to take a leak against the grey wall of the building.

"Someone told me you were happy," Pete said.

A cool breath of air blew across my eyes. His words lodged in a place in my brain that had been resting quietly.

"Who told you that?" I asked.

"It doesn't matter. Someone I used to know."

"Eileen?"

"Maybe not."

His voice was flat, with no inflections. I didn't remember it having been that way, with no rise or fall to it. Maybe it was heroin talk or prison talk or both.

"I've never been happy a day in my life," I said. "You should know that."

Pete twisted around on the bed till he faced me.

"How would I know that?"

My life was like a dusty old book to Pete, one that he'd never opened.

"Anyway, even if that was true," he said, "I heard that things had changed for you."

Three weeks ago Henry and I had sat on the patio at Carlos and Murphy's, drinking Coronas and eating nachos. It was late in the evening and though it was still light out, the sun was low and hidden behind the trees. My chair faced Osborne Street and as we talked and laughed I watched Eileen walk by on her own.

Henry was saying something funny. It was a story about his son, Dougwell, who was at the University of Toronto last year. Doug phoned Henry at work while he was teaching a class and told the receptionist that it was an emergency, to please get his dad for him. So Henry raced down the hall to the phone, expecting a severed limb at the very least, and found that Dougwell needed his dad's recipe for ribs. He was hoping to impress some friends on the weekend.

I hadn't seen Eileen notice us.

So Pete knew that Henry was here, and that we'd taken up together again.

I didn't mention Henry now; he didn't belong in this mess. I felt Pete's voice lodged in my own throat: *someone told me you were happy*. He couldn't stand hearing that information, so he came back to change it.

The Norwood Hotel has windows that open. But Pete's were all closed. I stood there for a couple of minutes, breathing the foul air, the filthy vegetable stench.

"What are you going to do?" I asked.

I had no idea what he was capable of; I didn't know him at all. Would it be a giant prank of some kind that would blow my life to smithereens?

He shrugged. "I don't know yet."

I didn't mention my burned-up garage. What if it hadn't been him that lit the fire? Pete didn't need any help from me coming up with ruinous ideas.

He didn't look able enough to pull off anything of consequence.

The whiskey wasn't going down well. I crossed the room and turned on the bathroom light. A hair dryer and an iron were attached to the wall. Everything in its place. I threw what was left of my drink down the sink.

There was nothing left to say. I paused at the door, considered begging Pete to leave me alone, and then thought better of it. When I closed the door behind me I wiped my hands on my cotton pants. I wished I had washed them.

The night was warm. I breathed heavily and my heart pounded in my ears. I wasn't ready to go home, so I sat in the park by the monument. That was where I had learned to smoke, as a kid. A girl named Katy taught me. She showed me how to inhale and how to let go of the cigarette while it was in my mouth so I wouldn't look like a nitwit.

Why had Pete invited me to come and see him? The visit hadn't accomplished anything. Maybe I didn't give him enough time to say what he wanted to say, but I had to get out of there.

What I had said to him about never being happy was a lie. There had been many happy moments in my life, even happy days. But I didn't want him to know that. I wanted him to know he didn't need to hurt me anymore. I'd had enough.

I read the words on the monument. The Korean War ended one year before I bit my brother on the cheek.

CHAPTER 29

I spent the following afternoon with Henry. He wanted to go the hotel to see Pete, to try to reason with him. He thought we could bring him around. That's how he put it.

"Bring him around to what?" I asked.

"To not doing anything more to scare you," Henry said, "or hurt you. I can't bear to think of you going there alone last night. You should have called me to go with you."

"I have a feeling this thing, whatever it is, is just between the two of us," I said.

"It doesn't have to be," said Henry. "I can help."

So we walked over to the hotel and knocked on the door of room 503. No one answered. We crossed the street to Pasquale's where we shared a small pizza. Neither of us was hungry. I drank a glass of house red and Henry a glass of white. We sat outside on the upstairs patio so that I could smoke comfortably. Then we tried Pete's room once more. Still no answer, so we checked with the woman at the front desk to make sure he was still registered and found that he wasn't.

"Did he leave you any indication of where he might be going?" I asked.

"No, ma'am, he did not."

"Uh, okay. Thanks."

"Great," said Henry.

"Maybe he's gone away," I said. "Maybe that was the last I'll ever see of him."

"I don't think so," said Henry.

We both knew he was right.

At ten o'clock the next morning, Tuesday, I was still in bed, but not asleep. I was stroking Spike's tummy, having decided that I'd get up when he did, but then the front doorbell rang. I leapt up and poked my head out the bathroom window, which overlooked the front street. It was Frank Foote.

"I'll be right down, Frank," I called out and he looked up at me and smiled. It was a worried smile, one that left creases between his eyebrows, so I expected the worst. I threw on a summer robe and hurried downstairs to the front door. Spike dashed ahead of me.

"Come on in," I said and we all went through to the kitchen.

I spilled some dry food into Spike's dish and changed his water. He nibbled away in appreciation, although it was his canned food later in the day that his life was geared toward.

"Cherry, I have some unsettling news for you."

"Yes."

"It's about Pete."

"Yes."

"A man has been found on the old Canada Packers grounds. He had Pete's identification in his pocket."

I sat down at the kitchen table.

"He's dead," I said.

"No. But he was unconscious when he was found."

"So he's okay?"

There was no denying my disappointment but I tried to keep it out of my voice.

"He's going to be, yes."

"Canada Packers?" I said. I pictured my brother lying there on the blood of long-dead cows.

"Yes."

"What's going on?"

"We don't know yet. Not for sure, anyway." Frank pulled out a chair and sat. "Apparently there was some evidence of drugs, so there's talk of an overdose that didn't quite do the job."

I remembered the painful-looking mess on the inside of Pete's arms.

"Also, there is a sizeable bump on his head."

"Where is he?"

"At Victoria Hospital," Frank said, "in intensive care."

"Have you seen him?"

"No. I'm going up there now. I could take you with me if you like, and bring you home again."

"Yes, okay."

I didn't want Frank to know that I had no desire to see my brother again, that I wished the overdose had taken. I didn't want him to think that I'm a terrible person. He makes me want to be good, like him.

Upstairs in the bathroom I washed my face and teeth, combed my hair, and put on my prettiest lipstick, Summer Berry. Then I dressed quickly in a pair of shorts that came down to my knees so there was no danger of anyone catching a glimpse of my thighs.

"Why Victoria Hospital?" I asked. "Why here?"

"They have space here." Frank said. "St. Boniface is full."

We were in a small room for ICU visitors. Frank talked briefly on a phone and then, after washing our hands at a sink near the door, we were allowed in to see my brother. With Frank being a policeman, I didn't even have to mention that I was Pete's sister. We approached the bed and I had the same experience I always have in hospitals. Every person in every bed looked very much like the person I'd come to see. Male, female, young, old—they all looked the same to me.

But there was no mistaking the man lying on his back with his eyes closed, tubes sticking out of him every which way, monitors beeping and flickering. There was a bruise on his arm, one bruise, on the sweet arm that my brother had tied off to inject his filthy west coast heroin.

"Henry," I said. And then blackness covered my eyes and I felt myself being buffered in my fall to the floor.

I think I woke up almost as soon as I passed out. Everything seemed as though it was part of the same moment that I left. I was in a chair now, though, and Frank was handing me a glass of water.

"Cherry?"

"Yes."

"Are you all right?"

"It's not Pete. It's Henry." I started to cry. "Henry Ferris."

"Yes," Frank said. "This is a real puzzler."

"No, it's not," I said.

"Pardon?"

I knew I had to do some talking but I wanted to find out about Henry first.

A nurse told us that he had been awake and that he was going to be fine. There would be no permanent damage from what had indeed been heroin injected into his arm. The needle had still been attached to him when a man out walking his dog found him at about 6:15 that morning. Also, he had suffered a concussion from a knock on the head.

Frank made a couple of phone calls.

Sure enough, Henry Ferris had been reported missing by his kids, so the whole identification mess got straightened out.

"It was strange that he only had one piece of ID in his pocket, no wallet or anything," said Frank.

"A giant prank," I said.

We headed out to the front lawn and found a grassy area where we sat. I told Frank about my visit with Pete at the Norwood Hotel. And I told him about Henry and me, how we'd rekindled our friendship after all these years.

"Yes, I figured that," said Frank.

When I cried he comforted me with his strong arms and his huge white handkerchief and his fragrant shirtfront.

"I sure cry a lot lately," I said.

"It's okay."

"Frank?"

"Yes?"

"When I asked Pete why he had come back now, he said it was because he had heard that I was happy."

"Oh?"

"I think he tried to kill Henry."

"Jesus, Cherry. His saying that doesn't necessarily mean that he is a would-be murderer," Frank said.

"I think it does."

We sat for a while, watching the traffic come and go, watching the patients with their IV's and oxygen tanks step outside for a smoke.

"Do we know when this was done to Henry?" I asked.

"Last night sometime."

"Early? Late?"

"Late. After dark for sure."

"So Henry wasn't out there alone for too long."

"I'm thinking it was in the wee hours of the morning," said Frank. "And don't forget, he wasn't conscious."

"Still. We don't know that, do we...that he was unconscious the whole time?"

"I guess we don't. We'll have to wait and talk to him."

"Henry and I went back to see Pete at the Norwood yesterday afternoon, but he had checked out."

"Cherry..."

"I know it was him, Frank. His ID was in Henry's pocket, for goodness' sake. He would have known that would fool us for about eight seconds. He isn't even trying for us not to know."

Frank shifted his position so he was lying on his side with his head resting on his hand. He looked good on the ground, as though he belonged there. I figured he probably spent a lot of time frolicking with his kids on a nice green lawn.

"I hope whoever it was meant not to give Henry enough of the drug to kill him," he said. "Making it more of a giant prank, as you said, than attempted murder."

"I don't know," I said.

"Maybe he's not as bad as you think," Frank said.

"I just don't know."

"Remember the way he used to be able to flip a coin across the tops of his fingers?" Frank said. "Just like a real magician."

"Yeah." I stood up, brushing little bits of grass from my knees. "Let's go in and look at Henry again before we go."

As we approached the waiting room I saw Dougwell and Gina Ferris sitting side by side on a couch. They were deep in conversation so they didn't see me. I yanked Frank's shirt and pulled him back out of sight.

"It's Henry's kids," I said. "I don't think we should interfere."

So Frank and I slipped out and left them to visit with their dad. It wasn't the time for me to burst upon the scene. I'd only met them a couple of times; they both seemed to like me well enough, but I was still a relatively new presence in their lives.

"Are the cops looking for Pete?" I asked as we cruised down Pembina Highway to Bishop Grandin Boulevard.

"I think we've pretty much decided to wait until Henry wakes up in a clearer state and then ask him about it."

"Hmph!" I said.

"We need more to go on, Cherry, than the relationship between you and your brother."

"And the ID in Henry's pocket."

"Yes. That's a good point."

I liked Frank, but once again, I found myself wondering if he wasn't a bit dim.

"How did they get to the stockyards?" I asked. "Pete doesn't have a car. Or maybe he does. I don't even know."

"Henry's car was reported missing along with Henry," said Frank.

I thought about this as we drove down St. Mary's Road.

"Do you mind if I stop in at St. Leon Gardens?" Frank asked as he pulled into their parking lot.

"I guess Pete must have gone to call on Henry," I said. "Taken a taxi maybe and then talked him into going for a ride."

Frank was out of the car and heading for the corn on the cob. I hurried along behind him. He bought a dozen and a half.

"My kids are maniacs when it comes to corn," Frank said. "Me too, actually." He smiled.

"Has Henry's car turned up?" I asked.

"No." Frank flipped out his wallet to pay for the corn.

"I bet it's somewhere in Norwood between the stockyards and my house," I said.

Frank looked at me, handed me his bag of corn and made another phone call.

"They found it already," he said when he hung up. "On Des Meurons, in the block just south of Marion. There was an iron on the front seat."

"An iron?"

"Yeah. A small one. It might be what caused the bump on Henry's head."

CHAPTER 30

In the late afternoon I decided to look for Pete. I walked through my neighbourhood to downtown Norwood. I hadn't eaten a thing all day. I noticed two yards with excellent crabapple trees; the apples were ready but I didn't think I could swallow anything at the moment. Maybe I'd pick some on the way home.

I walked down Marion Street, past the Norwood Hotel, past Al's Jewellers, the Legion, and the Dutch Meat Market, to the Dairi-Wip next to the Marion Hotel.

The Dairi-Wip Drive-In is famous for its burgers and fries. My stomach was growling but I had no appetite. I ordered a small vanilla ice cream cone to keep up my strength. I found a place to sit at an outside table with two burly bikers who were enjoying their Fat Boy burgers and their fries. One of them nodded at me; his mouth was full. The other guy was too busy with his food to acknowledge me. I licked daintily and consciously tried not to look like I was licking any part of a person.

It was a hot afternoon. The traffic built up on Marion Street as rush hour approached. I swallowed exhaust fumes along with my ice cream. When I was finished my cone I walked over to the hotel. The Marion was just the kind of place where Pete would feel at home and it wasn't far from where the cops had found Henry's car. Inside the cramped and darkened lobby a handsome young man sat behind a counter.

"Do you have a Peter Ring registered here?" I asked.

He smiled. "Is he a guest of the city?" His eyes were deep blue.

I didn't know what he meant at first.

"All of our guests are welfare recipients," he said. "They live here."

"Oh, I see. So there isn't anyone at all who would have checked in in the past day or two."

"No. Sorry," he said. "You could try the Chalet down the street."

"The Chalet. That's a good suggestion," I said and meant it. There are exotic dancers at the Chalet. Guys have been known to get beat up there. Plus, it was close to the stockyards where Henry was found.

My walk was turning out to be way too long. It wasn't that far to the Chalet from the Marion Hotel, but added on to the ground I'd already covered it was a fair distance. My walking sandals are comfortable and I was wearing one of my coolest dresses so I was feeling okay, but my hip was starting to ache. Back at the Dairi-Wip I asked for a large glass of water. I sat on the steps of the Ukrainian Catholic church across the street and drank it down.

I was fixing in my mind what I'd say to Pete if I found him, when I saw a familiar shape scuttling along the street heading east: Eileen. She didn't notice me. I followed her at a distance right to the Chalet. As I walked into the lobby I saw her disappearing up the stairs to the second floor. The young woman behind the desk grinned openly at me and I smiled back.

"How ya doin'?" she called out as I made my way quickly up the stairs.

She was as beautiful as the young man at the Marion was handsome. I wanted them to run away together to a land of clean air and fresh laundry.

On the second floor I took my time, listening at doors till I knew I had the right room. I heard Eileen's high-pitched whine and thought of Mitzi Widener.

"Let me get you something to eat, Pete. I'll go downstairs to the restaurant."

He murmured a reply.

"You really should eat something," she said.

"Let it go, Eileen." His voice was raised now.

I knocked on the door and opened it without waiting for a reply. Eileen was standing beside the bed where Pete sat slumped against the headboard. She was clutching a purse, looking more like she was shopping at Wal-Mart than visiting the junkie love of her life, sprung and free.

Pete dismissed her when he saw me. It wiped the smugness off her face and I took some satisfaction in that. She argued, but then left.

My heart was beating in my throat. What if he hit me on the head and stuck a needle in my arm? No. He'd have to take me by surprise and I wouldn't let him do that. Poor old Henry. He'd never have dreamed Pete would try to hurt him.

"You left the Norwood," I said.

"Good one," he said. He was agitated.

I poked my head in the bathroom. It was clean, with new fixtures.

Pete cooked up a mixture in a spoon.

"The 'Wood was too posh for me," he said. "The Chalet is more my style."

He pulled his lips back and they framed his rotting teeth. He rolled up a baggy pant leg to find a vein behind his knee.

I was grateful that he didn't pull his pants down, that I didn't have to see his underwear or worse.

Pete sank back on the bed with his eyes half-shut. A line of drool escaped one corner of his crusty lips.

I perched on a battered chair by the window. The curtains were closed. The only way I could keep from looking at the carpet and guessing what the stains were made of was to close my eyes.

Pete spoke in his monotone. "I knew he was dead when I was building my space ship. I just pretended I didn't."

My eyes opened and I saw a hint of a smile on his face.

"It was easier that way," he said.

He was talking about our dad.

"Murray," I said.

"Kind of like it was easier to pretend that I couldn't see you. Once I realized that people were so easy to fool, life became very simple for me."

He adjusted the pillows behind his head so that he was almost sitting up.

"No matter how much someone thinks they know you, they can never really fathom what's going on inside your head," he said. "No one can read anyone's mind."

"Did you mean to kill Henry?" I asked.

He closed his eyes for a long moment and then opened them abruptly and sat up.

"Of course not," he said.

"You could have."

"I could have baked a cake. I could have run naked through the streets of St. Boniface. There are many things I could have done."

"You know what I mean. You could have made a mistake with Henry and given him too much."

"No, I couldn't have; I'm a pro." Pete fussed with his lips, picking off pieces of non-existent fluff. "I like Henry," he added.

"You hit him on the head!"

"It was just a tap."

"No, it wasn't. He has a concussion."

"Concussion, shmoncussion." His eyes were at half-mast again, struggling to open wider.

"Let me bite you," he said.

"No!"

My heart stopped beating and I wondered if I was going to die. I wished I hadn't walked so far into the room. My heart must have been working because I made my way slowly toward the door.

"Come on," he said. "You owe me that much."

"I owe you nothing," I said, and repeated it over and over inside my head, to convince myself of the rightness of my statement.

My breathing was shallow. I struggled to get enough air. He knew about the bite. He had known all these years. Nora must have told him.

Pete snickered. "I remember it," he said, reading my mind, so soon after saying such a thing was impossible. "No one had to tell me."

I didn't try to speak; I needed all my energy to breathe.

He stood up and I could smell his chemical stink.

"Let me bite you," he said again. "Just once."

"No."

I backed toward the door and he lunged at me, but stumbled over a ripple in the carpet. He meant it. He wanted a piece of my flesh. I wondered if I could overpower him; I was pretty sure I could, wonky hip and all.

He crouched with his arms out to his sides like a wild man. When he lunged again I kicked him with my right foot and connected with the side of his face. I had a hand on each wall of the hallway to do that or I never could have managed it. A buckle on my sandal sliced his cheek open. Blood oozed down his face and he howled like a rabid wolf. He held his hand to the wound and slid down the wall to the floor. The blood ran fast enough to seep through his fingers. He didn't get up.

I closed the door behind me and ran the length of the hall and down the exit stairs. When I reached Coronation Park I was still shaking so I sat by the monument again until I calmed down.

How could he remember? He was only one. I supposed it was possible. Anyway, that didn't matter.

I walked home with Pete's words still buzzing through my brain.

His ignorance of my biting him, the circumstances of Murray's death, his not seeing me till I was nineteen, all those things that I had believed for my entire life turned out to be untrue. A lifetime of lies. All those basic facts of my existence disintegrated in a matter of moments. My whole childhood was wrong, a sham. In the newness of that information I had trouble not expanding the sham to include the whole of my life.

I favoured my aching hip on the way home and completely forgot about picking crabapples.

CHAPTER 31

In the evening Joanne and I went to see Henry. She drove. I didn't tell her about my visit with Pete. I was still digesting his words.

We pretended that I was Henry's wife and that Joanne was his sister. He wasn't conscious, but the nurse assured us that it was sleep, not a coma, and that he might be able to visit with us as early as the next day.

Back at my place Joanne stayed for one game of Scrabble. She won.

"Are you okay?" she asked as she dumped the tiles back into the box.

"Yeah. Why?"

"Well, all that's happened," she said. "Henry, Pete. You're very quiet. You didn't seem to mind my winning the game." She smiled. "That's not like you."

"I guess I'm okay. A little overwhelmed, I guess. Confused."

"Would you like me to stay overnight?" she asked.

I thought about that. It was a kind offer and I knew I should say yes. But I didn't. I said goodbye to my friend and did a little tidying up. Then I set myself up in the backyard to think about everything that was going on and to wait for whatever was going to happen next. I knew it wouldn't be long.

It was a bright and windy night. The shining moon and the streetlamp from the lane lit up the backyard like a stage. I sat in my camp chair sipping cool white wine from a glass. I smoked like a fiend. How could I not smoke while Pete was in my life? I decided I would give it up for a while after he was gone.

I looked at the air where my garage used to stand. The warm wind lifted up wisps of black ash from the pile of rubble and set them down again. There was nothing to be saved from the mess. The small building had always been more of a junk shed than a garage. I started to feel glad that it was gone.

Murray's hose reel stood apart and alone. I was pleased that it had survived the fire. I had reattached the hose.

Pete entered the yard through the gate and sloped toward me.

"Hello, Pete."

"Cherry."

It was still strange to hear him speak my name and to watch him see me.

He dragged one of Dougwell's wooden chairs over and sat. He reeked of sweat. All those new bathroom fixtures at the Chalet Hotel were going to waste. The blood had dried on his face but he had done nothing to clean it up. It was a nasty cut, on the same side as his scar, but lower down.

"What happened to the garage?" he asked.

"It burned down."

"I can see that."

It wasn't a topic I wanted to discuss.

"Drink?" I asked and showed him the bottle of La Playa.

"No thanks," he said. "I don't get much of a kick from drinking."

"Wait here." I got up. "There's something I have that I think you might like."

I locked the door behind me. If he were to come inside the house he might never leave. I could picture that.

Absinthe was what I was looking for. It's about six million per cent alcohol. A city councillor gave it to me as a gift when I interviewed him. He had brought it home from Prague. It came in a gift package with a bell-shaped glass and a perforated spoon for the sugar cube. It even contained wormwood, but not near as much as the absinthe from long ago. I had tried this modern version once. It had a strong licorice flavour with a slightly medicinal edge. Not unpleasant. It certainly didn't need the sugar. But I put all the supplies on a tray, including a pitcher of cool water. I knew the ritual would appeal to Pete and his romantic vision of himself. He could be buddies with Ernest Dowson and the other poets who had scarfed the stuff down in Paris in the 1890's. He could show them his haiku.

All I saw when I looked out the dining room window was my own reflection but I knew Pete was watching me. I thought about calling someone. Frank Foote? There wasn't a good enough reason. He and his cohorts didn't want any help from me with the Henry situation. Frank had made that clear enough. I hoped the police would have spoken to Henry by morning. That's when I'd call Frank.

Joanne would have dropped everything and been here in a minute, but to what end? There was a reason I sent her home. I wanted whatever this was to play itself out. I was pretty sure Pete wasn't going anywhere. He was home, after all. I'd see to it that he stayed till morning came.

When the tray was ready I considered spitting in the glass, like I'd heard disgruntled serving people do, then thought better of it. It would just be something I'd be ashamed of later.

The grass felt damp beneath my bare feet. I should have been wearing shoes with all that debris around.

"Haul that little table over, would you?" I said to Pete.

He did as he was told and I set the tray down.

"Absinthe," he said and smiled a lazy smile. His teeth, in that light, looked to be made of wood. His nose was running and his eyes were swimming in a viscous substance, something that wasn't tears.

He poured the green liquor into the glass and added sugar to the spoon. He dipped the sugar into the absinthe and out again and lit it with a match. It burned and bubbled till he plunged it back into the glass and the liquid was ignited.

I had the horrible thought that he was going to suck it into a syringe and shoot it up. But he added water then and the potion turned slightly cloudy. He took a swig and some of it dribbled down his chin and neck. So much for any ritual I'd ever heard of. "Why did you leave your ID in Henry's pocket?" I asked. "How could you have thought it would work for more than a few minutes?"

"It seemed like a fun idea," Pete said, "to pretend he was me. A few minutes, forever, what's the diff?"

He drank some more, didn't spill any this time.

"Fun," I said.

"Why didn't you ever leave this house?" he asked.

"I don't know," I said. "It's my home."

Pete sat for so long with his eyes closed that I considered going inside.

"It's my first memory," he said, as though he felt my intention and had to stop me. "You biting me, I mean. Why did you do that, Cherry?"

"I'm so sorry, Pete. I was a kid. Kids do stupid things."

"No need to apologize." He smiled. "It freed me up. Anything weird I did, or didn't do, was because of what you had done to me, at least as far as Nora and Murray and Dr. Bondurant were concerned. And I was even less on the hook by not remembering. If I'd admitted to having a recollection of it, I would have been blamed eventually for not being able to deal with it."

He finished what was in his glass and went through the whole routine again. This time the absinthe didn't flame when he stirred the burnt sugar into it.

"I used it forever," Pete said. "It never got old. And I learned early that you felt you deserved any punishment that came your way. I'm glad you bit me."

"My biting you wasn't near as bad as you trying to run over me with Nora's car," I said. "You were practically a grown-up when you hurt me. You could have killed me. Aren't you even a little bit sorry for doing that?"

"It was an accident," said Pete.

"Honest?"

"Yes."

It was what I wanted to hear, more than anything. So I believed it.

"You know Nora's dead," I said and poured the last of the wine into my glass. It wasn't going to be enough. I threw the empty bottle toward the rubble of the garage, wanting it to smash. But it just landed damply on the blackened grass.

He didn't acknowledge my mention of our mother.

"Being called Assface wasn't great," he said, "but really, it was just a bunch of letters run together to make a sound that wasn't all that unpleasant. Assface, Ashface, Assfish, Ashes."

I wanted to ask him about his new way of talking, in those even dead tones. But I stayed quiet.

"And it added to the sympathy that came my way, by adults especially, and even some of the kids, mostly girls."

Sitting back in my camp chair, I listened to him tell me that my whole life had been a mistake, based on his lies.

"I got so good at not seeing you," Pete said, "that I swear to Christ I didn't see you a lot of the time. I really didn't see you the night of the car accident, for instance, although I don't think anyone would have, with the light being off and all."

Mitzi Widener barked in her high-pitched voice. I welcomed its familiarity.

"I decided to be able to hear you," Pete went on, "because I was interested in what you said and also, I didn't want to work that hard.

"Not speaking to you was easy." He smiled. "I could pick and choose behaviours."

The absinthe wasn't making Pete drunk. He seemed to me to be in a state of calm lucidity. But I knew I couldn't count on that lasting.

"Dr. Bondurant told Nora that the trauma of having my sister bite me was compounded by Murray's death. The doc was a smart guy. A lot of the time he knew I was lying, but he couldn't get me to tell the truth. He felt powerless to help me. He told Nora that continued help would be good for me, that I should always have someone to talk to about my feelings so that I wouldn't act out in inappropriate ways. He even gave Nora the names of other psychiatrists, in case she or I wanted to try someone else, but she didn't bother. I seemed okay to her. My not seeing my sister didn't seem like a big deal to her. And yeah, I know she's dead. She let me know when she went into the hospital for the final time. She figured I should know that she was going to die."

"So she was in touch with you at Matsqui."

"Yup."

"She gave you her journal."

"Yup."

"You sent it to me this summer."

"Yup."

"Why?"

"I don't know. I thought you might find it interesting, I guess."

"Why now?"

"I was getting out."

"So?"

"I wanted to put you in the picture before…"

"Before what?"

"In case we lose touch."

I laughed. "Heaven forbid we should lose touch," I said.

"A nurse phoned me on the night that Nora died. Nora had confided in her about my being in jail and all. So she phoned to let me know."

"Dougwell didn't know about your situation," I said. I needed to be sure.

"No. Of course not."

It pissed me off when he said *of course not*, as if I could possibly take anything for granted.

"Why were you in jail for so long?" I asked. "The time seems long for the crime—selling drugs to kids, wasn't it?"

"That's what I got sent up for, but it's not what happened. I was buying, not selling."

"So Nora said in her clever code."

Pete chuckled. "Yeah, I knew you'd be able to figure it out."

"Why was the sentence so long?" I asked again.

"I became a full-fledged junkie in prison," Pete said. "That kind of promotes bad behaviour." He shivered.

The wind had calmed and the night was quiet without it. The atmosphere in the yard, where there had been fire so recently, was heavy like a dead weight, killed by the flames. I love quiet but not like that. It was like the calm before...what...Pete's next death?

"I phoned you that night," Pete said, "the night that Nora died."

"You did?" I was startled. "I remember the phone call I got that night."

"Do you remember what I said?"

"Yes."

"What was it?"

"You asked to speak to a nun."

Pete smiled and I did too.

"Sister Mary somebody or other."

"Mary of the Five Wounds," Pete said.

"Yes. That's it."

"That's Myrna's influence," he said. "We used to fool around on the phone all the time. She had some great lines."

A boatload of wine made an about-face and splashed up my esophagus to the back of my throat. I swallowed it.

"Myrna?"

"Yeah. We hung out for a couple of years before I went west."

"I didn't know that," I said.

"No. You weren't supposed to know. No one was. She was five years older than me and Eileen was my official girlfriend for part of the time, and Myrna thought you would kill her if you knew. There were lots of reasons for keeping it a secret."

"Pig."

"Who?"

"Myrna. You. Lying pigs."

Pete closed his eyes.

There were so many more questions I wanted to ask him, but they lost their importance next to Myrna.

"Did Myrna know you were alive all this time?" I asked.

But Pete was out; he'd gone limp.

In my basement I found a length of rope and I tied Pete to his chair. Then I tied the chair to the hose reel. He wasn't going anywhere.

He vomited in his sleep, coughed till his throat was clear. I waited for this to be over, to make sure he didn't die. I looked at the new wound on his face and the old scar higher up; it was barely there. Then I tied more knots to ensure that he would be there in the morning. That's when I'd call Frank.

I hadn't askedWe did talk about Diesel, the little beagle I had before Spike. Henry had been very fond of Diesel. And he said he was sorry, more than once; he just didn't say what for. Pete about Duane, if he'd set me up to be hurt. Maybe I would; maybe I wouldn't.

The car accident was an accident. That was important.

CHAPTER 32

I slept and dreamed that a Canada goose flew across the full moon. It seemed significant but I didn't know why. Its wings made a creaking sound as they flapped their way across. First I thought it was real and then I lay awake till I knew that it wasn't.

In the morning, I was up at first light. I wanted to take care of Pete before anyone walked down the lane and saw him. But I was afraid to look out the window, in case he was on fire or being eaten by wild dogs or worse.

I called Frank, not sure what to say.

"Pete is here." I settled on vagueness.

"I'll be right over," said Frank. "Just give me a minute to straighten things out around here."

"Okay."

I waited on the front lawn, shivering in the morning chill. He showed up within ten minutes.

We walked through the front hall to the kitchen, down the steps to the landing and out the door to the back stoop. Frank led the way.

"Oh my God," he said.

The first thing I saw was Pete's empty chair. It didn't seem possible to me that he could have freed himself. Then I remembered how he had put on magic shows in the neighbourhood. He could untie any knot anyone ever made. Pete was an escape artist, a magician. How could I have been so dull as to not think of that?

Then I saw a Green Guys truck parked in the lane with the engine running. A flash of anger darted through me as it always does when I see vehicles idling unnecessarily. Often they belong to the same people that won't allow smoking within one hundred yards of their dead relatives.

I didn't want to follow Frank's gaze. I didn't want to know why he had said, oh my God. But I looked and I saw an impossible embrace—green coveralls wrapped around and lifting up a limp scruffy body. The coveralls let go quickly as the man inside them realized what he was hanging on to.

The scarecrow was left to swing in the brittle wind.

It was made from the rubble of my garage and from armfuls of old vegetation, encased in bits of cloth. Glancing around my yard, I could see there was no shortage of junk to fashion this type of decoy. Pete could have built a family of scarecrows.

"I thought," stuttered the Green Guy, "I'm sorry, I thought someone was…"

He blushed as though he had made an unforgivable mistake.

"No. Don't worry," Frank hurried down the steps and over to where the Green Guy stood. He put his hand on the man's shoulder. "Don't apologize. You did the right thing. I thought the same thing as you did when I saw it."

I stepped down into the yard. "Here, sit," I said, and offered him my camp chair.

He dropped into the chair. "I was driving down the lane and I seen someone hanging."

"I understand," I said.

He looked straight at me. "I'm sorry," he said.

It was the same Green Guy who had tried to trick me into having my lawn aerated. The same guy I had decided to hate for his underhandedness. I've made that kind of mistake before—despising someone who gave of himself in an entire kind of way. Misplaced hate. Hate with a shallow reason.

The scarecrow had a noose around its neck. When I looked closely I saw that Pete had made it out of the rope that I had bound him with. And he had used the hose and toppled Dougwell's chair.

I realized that the creaking of the goose's wings in my dream was the sound made by Murray's hose winder.

Pete had fashioned a pocket on the scarecrow's burlap shirt and attached a pen, the way both Murray and Dougwell used to do. The way Frank does. There was a piece of paper in the pocket, torn from a small ringed notebook, the kind Pete always used to carry for his haiku. I guess he still did. There were a few words written in my brother's awkward hand:

> *four ewe*
> *in morning light*
> *only 4 u*

That's what he wrote: a fucked-up haiku.

I pocketed the poem without showing Frank. He saw me do it but didn't ask. He knew it was between my brother and me.

The Green Guy left. Frank stuck around for a while, cut down the scarecrow. We talked some. I told him about my visit to Pete at the Chalet, our scuffle.

"He tried to bite me," I said.

"Jesus."

"Yeah."

I told Frank about my brother's admission that he had hurt Henry and that got him moving.

"He didn't intend to kill him," I called after Frank as he crossed my front yard.

That brought him to a stop and he turned around.

"He said so," I said.

Frank nodded and continued down the block.

I made coffee and sat with the crumpled scarecrow as the dewy morning heated up.

Somehow, Pete knew that his repeated deaths were the best way to get to me. My life was a ghastly treasure hunt that I was on against my will. Pete's dead body was the prize, but it was a booby prize; it was never real.

Frank called soon after to tell me that Pete was no longer registered at the Chalet. He asked if I had any other ideas. I gave him Eileen's address. Not Myrna's. I still didn't believe what my heart knew was true.

CHAPTER 33

By the time I got up to see Henry in the afternoon he had been moved to a private room on another ward. He had already told his story twice, once to a young cop in a uniform and once to Frank, who was there shortly before I was.

Henry was ghostly white underneath his tan and that made him look old, but he insisted that he felt okay.

"Just tired," he said. "I can't seem to get over wanting to roll over and go back to sleep."

I didn't want to push him, but I was desperate to hear what had happened.

"Pete came to see me," he said. "I would have said last night, but apparently it was the night before. I lost a day in there."

"I'm so sorry," I said.

"It's not your fault," he said. "Anyway, it was late. I was already in bed. So were Dougwell and Gina. They didn't wake up, thank goodness."

"Maybe it would have been good if they had," I said.

"No."

Of course not. Henry didn't want his kids tainted by Pete Ring. Would we be able go on from here at any level? I wondered. The same blood runs through me as through the guy that could have killed Henry.

"He wasn't trying to kill you," I said. My brother's advocate.

"I know. The doctor said it wasn't enough to even hurt me. I guess I'm extra susceptible or something. I just slept an extremely deep sleep for a very long time."

"How did Pete know where to find you?" I asked.

"He just looked me up in the phone book."

I smoothed his hair back from his forehead. "You should have an unlisted number, Henry, being a teacher. Don't you have students phoning you all the time?"

"No, not really. Sometimes. It's never bothered me."

"Okay, so what next?"

"He asked if we could go for a ride in the Volvo. He was a little wild-eyed, so I figured that would be better than inviting him in. I didn't want the kids to see him."

"No. Of course not."

"Cherry? Are you okay?" Henry took my hand.

"Yes."

His fingers were chilly and I rubbed them briskly and kissed them and put them down.

"Saying no to him didn't seem to be an option," Henry said, "so I got dressed while he stood outside in the yard. I was hoping he'd be gone by the time I got back, but he was there, all right. He had a jacket on, which I thought was unusual because it was a warm night. It didn't occur to me that that'd be where he was hiding all his stuff: the iron, the fixings."

"The iron."

"Yeah. That's what he hit me with."

I pictured the small iron attached to the bathroom wall at the Norwood Hotel. Had he stolen it in order to use it on Henry? Or was there a similar iron situation at the Chalet? I hadn't noticed. It didn't matter.

"So we cruised around for a while. I drove. I thought he would talk, but he didn't. And I couldn't think of anything to say. There were things I was curious about: jail, being a drug addict, faking death. But they didn't seem like appropriate topics." Henry chuckled. "That sounds ridiculous, I know."

"No, it doesn't," I said.

"So, anyway, he finally told me to drive down Archibald to where Canada Packers used to be. He wanted me to pull right onto the site, which I did, by driving around to the back. There was a section where the fence had collapsed. By this time I was getting a little uneasy."

Henry sipped water through a straw. I wondered why the straw was necessary. It made him seem so frail.

"Remember how the air in Norwood used to smell like… livestock sometimes," he said, "if the wind blew in a certain way?"

"Yes. Dead livestock, I think."

"Maybe. Anyway, I could smell it there. It was very unnerving. It probably would have seemed less so if there had been some conversation but he was so quiet. And every time I spoke my voice got higher and higher so I shut up. I parked where he told me to and then caught a glimpse of the iron when I turned toward him. That's all I remember."

Henry touched his head gently where he had been hit.

I thought about how knocks on the head sometimes killed people and I shuddered.

"Oh, Henry. No one deserves to be hit with an iron less than you do."

He smiled and reached for my hand again.

"Pete's 's in terrible shape,.." he said.

"Yeah," I said. "I think the next time he dies it might be for real."

"Where is he, Cherry?"

"I don't know. The cops are looking for him though. They'll find him soon. He doesn't try very hard to hide anything anymore."

There would be time enough in the days to come to fill Henry in on all the things that Pete was no longer hiding.

"Frank said that a man out walking his dog found me. I guess Pete dragged me out of the car and left me there. They found the car on Des Meurons, so he must have driven it that far."

"Yes."

"I feel as though I'm going to drift off again," said Henry. "I don't want to. I keep dreaming about my heart."

"Your heart?"

"Yeah. Like it's burning up or frozen solid or melting or running away."

Henry was asleep again.

"Is his heart okay" I asked a nurse who stopped in to check on him just as I stood up to leave.

"Whose heart?"

"Henry Ferris' heart," I said and pointed to him in the bed.

She assured me, after scanning all his paperwork and Henry himself, that yes, his heart was fine.

I hoped she wasn't lying or mistaken.

After a dish of butterscotch pudding in the hospital cafeteria I checked on Henry again. He was still asleep, so I left him a note and caught a bus home.

CHAPTER 34

It was 6:30 p.m. and I stared into the open fridge. There wasn't much to choose from. Finally I chose a small can of beans from the pantry, put them in a pot and set them on the stove to heat.

The phone rang.

It was Myrna. I turned the heat off under the beans.

"Can you come over?" she whispered.

"Why are you whispering?" I asked.

"I think you'd better come over."

"Why?"

"Pete's here."

Paranoia swept through me. Everyone knew more about my brother than I did. I couldn't bear Myrna being in this picture.

"Cherry?"

"Yes."

"Please come."

"Is he dead?" I pictured him laid out on one of her slabs, waves of stink rising from the body.

"No. He's not dead. Just come, will you? Take a taxi. I'll pay for it."

I dialled 775-0101 for a Duffy's cab. Then I grabbed Frank's phone numbers off the dining room table where he had left them. I tried his home phone first. He answered on the first ring.

No one ever goes to Myrna's place voluntarily. Dead people live there.

She met me at the curb and paid the driver.

We didn't go in the front door to the house. We walked around to the side and entered there, into a short hallway that smelled like the science lab at Nelson Mac on the day that we dissected frogs. I threw up that day. I had known it was coming and ran down the hall to the boys' washroom. It was closer than the girls'. I made it to a sink before I spewed my guts. There was just one boy at a urinal. He was out of there before he had time to give his dick a shake.

Now we entered a large white room with four tables, four slabs: the room where Myrna does her work. There was a fridge, a freezer, two stainless steel sinks, water-glass fronted cupboards, spotless countertops. Three of the tables were empty. On the fourth there was a slight figure underneath a heavy sheet.

Pete stood at one end of that table. He had lifted the edge of the covering and he was looking at the dead body.

"Get away from there!" Myrna hissed.

Pete jumped back.

"What's she doing here?" he asked.

"I called her," Myrna said.

"What for?"

Myrna sighed. She was wearing orange lipstick. Like on the glass in Pete's room at the Norwood.

I hate orange lipstick.

It was Myrna that Pete was in touch with all through the years, not Eileen. It was Myrna who told Pete I was happy.

"You knew he was alive," I said. I wasn't able to look at her. "All this time, you knew."

"She and Eileen both knew," said Pete. "So what?"

I turned to him. "Are you going to kill me?" I asked.

"No."

"Or hurt me physically in any way?"

"No," said Pete. "Of course not." His gummy eyes wandered.

Of course not. My face was heating up, but I struggled to stay calm.

"Or Henry?" I asked

"No." Pete snickered. "I've already done Henry. How is he, by the way?"

"None of your business."

Pete had lost a front tooth since the night before. He was falling to pieces.

"What are you going to do next?" I asked.

He reached out for a straight wooden chair, dragged it noisily across the white tile floor and sat down.

"You talk like I have a master plan," he said. "I'm just taking it minute by minute. Believe me."

"Believe you?"

"Yeah. Why not?" He smirked.

"Okay," I said. "Give me your best shot. Die every day if you want to. That seems to be what you do best. I can take it."

There was a knock at the door and Myrna went to answer it. Frank came in and took Pete outside. I didn't know if anyone but me realized how useless this all was. There was no way Henry would press charges against my brother. And he hadn't really done much else, except steal an iron, drive Henry's car a few blocks, use drugs and try to bite me. Would the cops be able to charge him without any input from Henry? I doubted it. There was possible arson; that was something. But they'd need proof. Maybe he would admit to it.

I followed them outside and Myrna came too.

"Cherry?"

I didn't answer.

"Cherry, please," she said.

I still didn't answer.

She went back inside. I guess it was time to get started on the stiff.

Frank and Pete and I sat on the front lawn of the funeral home in the shade of a Manitoba maple. It was evening now and the sun was low. The days were getting shorter. Frank asked Pete why he had been given such a long sentence for his drug bust in British Columbia.

"Bad behaviour," Pete said, like he did when I asked him.

"Did it have anything to do with the 1981 riots?" Frank asked.

"Yeah, some," Pete said. "I was due to get out that summer. And then the riots happened. I got caught up."

"What riots?" I asked.

"There were riots at Matsqui in June of '81," Frank said. "The place was in flames. It was all over the news at the time."

It rang a faint bell.

"So when did you finally get out?" Frank asked.

"Not till early this year." Pete grinned. "I just couldn't seem to behave myself."

He reached in his mouth and came out with a dark brown tooth. He tossed it at the trunk of the maple tree.

"After the riots I got into junk pretty heavily. It wasn't hard to get fixed up inside. I would get caught up every now and then and the time just kept stretching out."

"How could you and Nora have thought it was a better idea to pretend that you were dead than admit that you were in jail?" I asked.

Pete laughed and it turned into a cough. "How can you even ask that?" he said. "It was all about appearances for Nora. All. I couldn't have given a flying fuck if Jane Fonda knew I was in jail, but Nora couldn't handle it. It was just too shameful. She said, how could you do this to me? about eight thousand times."

It was the most animated I had seen him since he came back. It took our goddamn mother to get a rise out of him.

"She wa-ay preferred my death."

My eyes began to ache. How many times do I have to weep for my brother? I didn't want to do it then, in front of him. I forced the tears back and the ache got worse.

Frank took Pete to the Remand Centre but he was out in a couple of days. He wouldn't admit to the arson and Henry made it clear that he just wanted to forget about the whole thing.

His kids were furious. They wanted Pete strung up. Henry hadn't told them that the maniac who had hurt him was my brother. He made up a name, Buzz Mantle, and a story about an old rivalry from the past. A rivalry for a history scholarship. It was the best he could do in his weakened state. He didn't want them to associate anything bad with me.

I'm a little uncomfortable with this fabrication but I'm glad that Henry wants to protect me and what we have together, although I'm still not sure what that is.

Henry is not the love of my life, but I don't think I'm going to have one of those.

CHAPTER 35

The next time I saw Pete he was laid out at Myrna's place on one of her tables. This time he really was dead.

Frank knocked on my door the Friday morning before the long weekend, to tell me that Pete had washed up on the bank of the Red near the Provencher Bridge. Two nuns out for a walk saw his body knocking up against the river's edge.

"Did he jump or did he fall?" I asked.

"I don't know, Cherry. I'm sorry."

"Maybe he was pushed," I said.

"I don't know."

"What were the nuns' names?" I asked.

"I don't know that, either. I'm sorry."

Pushed, fallen, jumped. I could pick whichever one sat best with me. The police ended up ruling it a drowning by misfortune, an accident. There had been no evidence of foul play.

Now it was Monday, Labour Day, and I was with my brother in Myrna's death room. She had left us alone and Frank waited outside.

Myrna had done a pretty good job of fixing him up. He looked dead all right, absent, but not scary or gross. I touched the twin scars on his cheek; the old one barely visible and the new one still a scab. Myrna had tried to cover it. I found some cotton swabs and alcohol in a cupboard and removed the makeup hiding the angry quarter moon. He was going to be cremated, but still, I didn't want it hidden.

I half expected his eyes to flutter open. Just another lark. But they didn't. I am so glad that they found him, the nuns. What if he had never washed up and I spent the rest of my life looking over my shoulder for him?

It turned out the nuns had regular names: Valerie and Margaret. They don't seem to take on dramatic titles anymore, like Sister Mary of the Five Wounds. I was disappointed in a low-key kind of way.

I chose to believe that Pete fell. I didn't want him to have given away whatever remained of his deathly life.

If only I had been able to embrace him, if only I hadn't bitten him. Maybe he had been counting on me. Maybe he had known Murray was doomed and that Nora couldn't love him in the way he needed.

Did Pete escape guilt? Did he feel so wronged that his own vengeful acts left him feeling scot-free? Or was the guilt buried so deep that it festered inside his bones and sickened him? Like Nora's smothered true self had done to her.

Frank drove me home and sat with me awhile on the front steps. My backyard was still a disaster area. Whoever was supposed to show up to clean away the remains of the fire hadn't managed it yet.

We drank lemonade. It was hot in the sun, but fall was beginning to make its presence known in the odd golden leaf drifting down in my peripheral vision.

"It was the fellow from Green Guys who burned down your garage," Frank said.

"Hmm," I said. It occurred to me that I may never feel surprised about anything again in my whole life.

"He came by the morning of the scarecrow to check out his handiwork."

I pictured him hugging and lifting the semblance of a man that Pete had concocted.

"Not a very successful criminal," I said.

Frank chuckled. "No. He blurted it out to me when he was doing my next-door neighbour's lawn. We were talking about something completely unrelated, the scarecrow, I think. You had apparently pissed him off in some way. He didn't realize I was a cop. I had to arrest him then and there. Arson is a serious crime."

"I guess you're the type of person people blurt things out to," I said.

"He's done it before, too," Frank said. "This was not a first offence."

"I'm pleased it wasn't Pete," I said.

"Me too," said Frank

I was pleased, too, that I could feel less guilty now about my knee-jerk hatred of the Green Guy.

After Frank left, I phoned Dougwell Jones to tell him that Pete was dead. I told him the choices that we had to pick from: leapt, fell, or pushed. I told him that for now I was going with fell. But even as I said it I realized that I didn't believe it anymore. Pete had jumped and a piece of me believes that a small part of him may have done it for me.

Dougwell knew about my older sister who died, the one I read about in Nora's journal. Nora had told him. And he knew that the little body of Baby Girl Ring was buried in St. Vital Cemetery. He didn't know why my mother hadn't buried Murray's ashes out there beside her. Maybe I would like to do that now, he suggested.

I phoned the cemetery and made the necessary arrangements, to bury both my father's ashes and those of my brother beside the long-dead body of Baby Girl Ring. In my head I named her Luce.

As soon as I hung up the phone rang. It was Dougwell. He still had Nora's ashes, he said, in an urn in a cupboard. He offered them to me.

"Yes, " I said. "I'll take them. I'll place them with the others."

I phoned the cemetery back and postponed the burial.

CHAPTER 36

I'm done with my column, *No, But Really*. I went to see my editor at the *Free Press* to tell her that I am no longer able to write it. She didn't seem at all disappointed. I told her that I'd been tossing around a couple of ideas for a different kind of column and she was genuinely interested in a change of tack. That was a relief; I didn't want to worry that they didn't want me at all. I needed a break, though, and I told her that. I had a train ride to take and many things to ponder. She didn't even try to get me to tell her about my new ideas. I was grateful for this, as I hadn't sharpened them up yet.

I knew that I no longer wanted to hurt people with my words.

One of my ideas was a column about things that happen to the human body and mind as you age. I would get things rolling by talking about my second hip replacement. People could write to me about their strange growths and odd-coloured rough patches: the things their doctors tell them to stop worrying about. They could tell me about their hair going from poker straight to curly or about how they sprouted an extra asshole over the long summer.

I dreamed that a man wrote to me about an insect growing out of a sore on his face. I told him to wash and I didn't use it in my column. He didn't like this and came after me. I forced myself awake so I wouldn't have to meet him face to face. My sheets were soaking wet and I decided that that idea for a column was foolish.

My other concept also concerned aging, but it had to do with discoveries that come with age, bits of wisdom that people might like to share. I could call it *Good Stuff to Know* or *What a Good Idea!*, something like that. I would start out with my own bits of wisdom that I knew were none too wise, but that would let people know that their views didn't have to be genius calibre to share. Things like: after a night of too many cigarettes, take a brisk walk, breathing deeply and you won't feel nearly as horrible the next morning. It's true! You just have to force yourself to do it.

And people could send in questions: Does anyone sell fruit you can count on? Do our teeth grow further apart as we get older? Why don't men have trouble with their thighs? What, once and for all, is the truth about worms? And other readers could write in answers, theories, comforts.

This one seemed more likely—an interactive column—a friendly, positive column. I could maybe fit a few bits from my first idea in, but in a helpful way: what to do if you find yourself drooling while awake, or breathing loudly on the bus, or drifting off at parties.

CHAPTER 37

I'm on a train going west to see Dougwell Jones. Joanne and Henry saw me off. As the train pulled out of the station I noticed that Hermione had arrived as well. No sign of Myrna. I haven't seen or spoken to her since the day I picked up Pete's ashes. I doubt if we can still be friends; I'm not sure we ever were. This is one of the many things I have to think about during my trip to Penticton.

"I loved you both. What was I supposed to do?" she asked the last time I saw her.

You loved Pete more, I thought. Yet how could I blame her for that?

But still.

Another thing I have to think about is the trip Henry and I have decided to take to Ireland next summer. Henry still loves me after all that has happened. He says it is impossible that he would stop loving me, that no one could love me more than he does.

And I'm still not sure how I feel about Henry. I love him for sure, but it ebbs and flows, just like it did when we were young. Next summer might be too far away to plan.

Spike is in good hands. Joanne is looking after him at her house and she won't let him off his leash while I'm away. He and her dog, Wilson, get along pretty well. Frank offered to take Spike too, so I know I have a backup dog sitter.

Soon there is no trace of the city outside the window.

The train reminds me of the one my dad would travel on when I was a girl. While we waited for it to rumble in from Regina, where Murray had gone to visit his sister Ruth, Pete and I would play on the Countess of Dufferin steam locomotive outside the CPR Station. Nora smoked nearby. Then, when we heard the train coming, we went into the station and climbed the long stairway that led up to it. At the top of the stairs, we were outside again. I peered through the cold steamy morning till I saw Murray's familiar form loping towards us. And then I ran. He dropped everything to crouch down and hold me while I pressed my face into the rough cloth of his overcoat.

"How's my girl?" he always said.

But it's me now, on board, travelling through the prairie afternoon in mid-September. I sink into the comfort of the leather seat and smile at the elderly gentleman across from me. The sun slants through the windows and glints off the chain on the old man's watch.

The breeze dances in the tall grass as the train rolls by, blowing its horn at each town and village along the way: Carberry, Elkhorn, Wapella, Indian Head. The smell of sweet clover mingles with the oil and smoke from the train. And apples. A woman passes through with a basket of dusty apples that fill the air with their scent. She moves from one car to the next, the heavy doors clanging shut behind her. I want very much to bite into one of those sweet apples.

Henry offered to come with me but I want to go alone. It will give me a chance to know Dougwell better. He is, after all, family of sorts.

After I visit Dougwell I will come home to Jane and Spike and Hermione and Henry. To Dr. Bondurant—I made an appointment with him that I'm going to keep. (He still has a part-time practice.) To a date in November to have my new hip installed. I won't be laid up for as long as I was the first time around. To my brand-new column. And I'll have a proper burial for the members of my family. Friends will come and I'll say my good-byes. Once and for all.

ABOUT THE AUTHOR

Alison Preston was born and raised in Winnipeg. After trying on a number of other Canadian cities, she returned to Winnipeg where she lives with her partner Bruce and their cat in Norwood Flats. A graduate of the University of Winnipeg, and a letter carrier for the past twenty-six years, Alison has been twice nominated for the John Hirsch Award for Most Promising Manitoba Writer, following the publications of *The Rain Barrel Baby* (Signature Editions) and *A Blue and Golden Year* (Turnstone Press), also literary mysteries.

THE RAIN BARREL BABY

ISBN 0921833-83-0

Inspector Frank Foote's normally quiet neighbourhood, Norwood Flats, is greening into summer when a dead baby is discovered in his neighbour's rain barrel. The tiny body has evidently been in the rain barrel for some time, and there are no obvious leads in the case. Frank's seen a lot of crime scenes, but this one is a little too close to home.

Meanwhile, Gus Olsen, who made the gruesome discovery, is a little worried about the mysterious woman who has been cruising Claremont Avenue in her Lincoln Town Car. He's been meaning to talk to Frank about her, but he doesn't want to bother the inspector, who already has his hands full trying to take care of his three children while their mother dries out in an addiction treatment centre.

Frank is a good father, he tries to be a good husband, and he hopes he is a good cop. But, like all of us, Frank has a few old secrets that he is ashamed of. And before this summer ends, Frank will have to confront his past.

THE GERANIUM GIRLS

Beryl Kyte, a letter carrier who lives in the Winnipeg neighbourhood of the Norwood Flats, goes out for a hike one beautiful spring Saturday and literally trips over a body in the woods of St. Vital Park. It's a dead woman with mushrooms sprouting in her mouth. A badly shaken Beryl is questioned and escorted home.

ISBN 0921833-83-0

It isn't long, however, before another body turns up and then another. As she follows the horrific discoveries in the local newspaper, Beryl thinks she sees a pattern emerging. She hadn't been of much help to the police in the case of the first dead woman—she'd only tripped over the body, after all— but when things begin happening around her own home, she wishes they could be of some help to her. But she can't even make the call, for the crimes taking place in her yard—someone has been deadheading her lobelia and someone has put a pretty little collar on her cat— will just make the police think she's crazy. Except maybe that nice Inspector Frank Foote.